SUSAN M. CONWAY

A Life of Whoredom

Contents

Preface

Who am I?

Perhaps we are all lost in translation; roaming amuck like starving beasts, searching for this ever elusive ancient manual that gives us the step-by-step instructions of the processes to one's own *unbecoming*. We are born, and before our feet ever have the opportunity to touch the ground, we get muddied by trauma; and those of us that were left to develop our own set of coping skills into adulthood, we get glorious-filthy sex that anesthetizes the pain of becoming the collective, 'They.'

* * *

Becoming, society...

We decide in our fumbling flailing that conforming is the path of least resistance in the short term, so we lose sight of and give up on our futures to work tirelessly to become bearable and tolerable to the world; we seek to become palatable, and to be capable of bearing. And, all of it for what? You traded your chance at a kingdom for a barren wasteland of recycled thought processes and stale experiences that will never take you any further than the locked fence that is conformity and normative socialism.

Experience paired with an open mind, soul, and body are keys to a kingdom filled with riches beyond your wildest imaginations. For, to gain experience is to be fully human; and to be fully human is to **know** you are a Universe that is experiencing and manifesting itself through you, over and over, every day, and in every way that it possibly can.

The herd mentality is toxic, it is dangerous, and it is assuredly a self-imposed death sentence of the spirit. I was there once; I wanted to fit in, 'be normal', not make waves... And then, one fateful day a long time ago, someone left the gate open, and I was frightened, but once I started toward this scary world outside of the prison I had built around myself, I realized it wasn't anything to be afraid of, rather it was an invite into a new world. I began to run, and I ran, and ran, and ran, as fast and as far away as I could from the indoctrination that was my history. I leapt into the arms of beasts and men, and sailed seas built of my tears both happy and sad, I fucked lessons and blessings, and sometimes, the both of them were all wrapped up into one open gate, one unlocked door...

Once I realized that *living* life was an invitation out of my cage, I exploded into life and my truth like a supernova. It was only when I had cast fear aside and pushed forward that I understood-existence was a locked gate around a barren wasteland. And, that so many of my fellow human beings are still, to this day, wandering about aimlessly in. They are depending upon and eating the scraps society is handing them through the holes in the fence.

* * *

Since my new-found freedom, I have experienced and manifested the fuck out of myself and some other gorgeous celestial bodies that set themselves free.

They said YES to the invite.

Now, here we are, out here, groping our way through each other's cosmos. My atmosphere is all carbon dioxide and heavy breathing, dizzy, disoriented heavenly boulders of bodies crashing into and happening upon each other. My Universe is electrical storms, and wet and dry seasons, and to know me is to experience me. So, if 'who am I' is your question, I encourage you to read this book from start to finish; journey along with me in my unbecoming and the unearthing of the woman I have become. You never know, you just might find the answers to questions you never knew you had within the pages of this novel. Perhaps, you will begin to deeply ponder what it is that your Universe consists of, and how you might begin to manifest the truth of *who it is* that you are unbecoming into. Here I am, opening the gate for you. It is an invite, not a threat to your existence. I want to tell you, now that you are at the gate, peering out into the wilderness, it's nice to see that you have pushed fear aside, and put in the work to show up. Now, let's see you rise to the occasion of arriving, my friend. Run, and run, and run, you fucking majestic beast.

If your fear is that you are an isolated little island and that you will not be understood if you find your truth and begin the work to live fully in it, I assure you, you aren't alone. There are others, and we can do this life together. All you have to do is say Yes to the invite; but more importantly, step through the gate, and by doing so, you say Yes to yourself, the most important person in this excruciatingly stunning moment.

In this moment, you are neither too much nor too little of anything. In this moment, you are glorious, and beautiful, and brave, and mighty. You are capable, and willing, and I accept you as you are. You are so worthy of this opportunity. We have been waiting for you without judgement, in perfect love, and in perfect trust.

My fellow human being, I say to you, welcome, welcome, welcome. Your Kingdom awaits, just outside these walls.

-S. *Conway*

Acknowledgement

To all whom have been a lesson or a blessing in my life; I honor you. To the women who helped me make this book possible, my deep gratitude and appreciation.

-Susan M. Conway

1

Chapter 1

There is a deeply wounded animal that resides within me. And it wails and hisses, and smears its hands down this pretty, sad face of mine, in agony. I just get so sick of myself sometimes. I get so tired of teetering on the edge of sanity; one stiff wind and I am going off the deep end. There was no normal once Lucas appeared in my life; not that there ever was a great measure of normalcy in my life before him. I was severely abused by my parents, and they were addicts who came from a long line of abuse and addiction. I was a child of the system; the state took my sisters, my brother, and myself and placed us in foster homes where children were nothing more than a paycheck and extra hands to take the burden of domestic duties off the adults. My head was held under water in a toilet soiled with feces, and urine, and mold from every member of the foster care household; the kids would not let me up until I drank from it.

We were the abandoned, the beaten, the rejected, and the marked. I don't blame them, I don't hate them; not the abusers and not the victims who chose to become their own versions of their predecessors. We were all groomed from a very young age to perpetuate this vicious toxicity that is falling in love with walking traumas. I get it, I do... I forgive them all, and I forgive myself. I forgive myself for the abuse, the abandonment, and the rejection of myself. I have been far worse to myself than any ass whoopin' I took from my mother and father, partner, and friend. There isn't one person roaming this earth that could say or do anything worse to me than what I have already said and/or done to myself. And to myself, I say, "I am sorry. I will do much better by you, because you deserve to be treated with love, honor, respect, and dignity."

It just took me a while to realize that. But now that I understand this, now that I have taken this into my spirit as truth, no one gets to take that away from me. That is powerful, I am powerful. Had these things not happened to me, I fear the human being I would have become. Because I have had my ass handed to me seven ways from Sunday, I have had to fight tooth and nail to become the woman I am today.

* * *

I was adopted out as a baby, with one of my sisters, to a family that had managed to fly under the government's radar in regard to the standards and laws that must be upheld in order to adopt, as once again, I found myself in the midst of an abusive, drug, and alcohol addicted home. My sister took many beatings to protect me; I will forever be grateful and heartbroken over it. My adoptive mother and step father's cruelty knew no bounds. At the age of sixteen, my sister ran away from home, leaving me to receive the brunt of their wrath. A couple years later, after my mother had abandoned me to go elsewhere to live her life, away from my alcoholic step father (with whom I was then living), I also ran away at sixteen years old.

I ran into the arms and home of my high-school sweetheart, thinking his love would protect me, that our love would conquer and heal all, that we would marry, and I would be the best wife there ever was. We got engaged, I married him and was pregnant by the age of seventeen, I had my son at eighteen years old, my husband and I separated legally by the time I was nineteen, and we divorced by the time I was twenty. Life was a whirlwind, and the experience of becoming a runaway, a mother, a wife, and attempting to care for all of these needs wasn't anything

I was even remotely close to being ready for. Neither of us were emotionally and mentally equipped to contend with transitioning into marriage and children; we were babies having a baby, we were doing adult things we had no business doing.

It was a tumultuous time, to say the least.

I did what I had always done best when things got frightening, I ran away, and I hid from the hurt and the scary. I buried my feelings and refused to face them until the time came that life demanded of me I either jump into the abyss of healing and unbecoming, or I will be dragged and pushed. I chose to be dragged.

And here is what happened, once over the cliff:

* * *

I was a cocktail waitress at a small watering hole on the East Coast. The bar was packed, shoulder to shoulder; standing room only, on a Friday night. I served him his Gin and Tonic and he shot me a sideways smile and boldly made direct eye contact. I melted into a bubbling mess of whatever substance he desired me to be. There were fan girl shrieks from every fiber of my being-but mostly, from my vagina.

I know he said, 'Thank you.' I saw his lips mouth the words before the sound waves hit my ears like sonic booms. My insides shook, and I almost dropped the tray I had woven my way through the sea of bodies carrying. I fumbled a bit and managed a very shaky, "Y-you're welcome," before turning crimson and making a quick but awkward getaway back to the bar.

I sat the tray down and focused on breathing. The bartender, Chad, smiled and slid over a glass of ice water. I smiled back wearily and muttered, "Thanks."

"It's that rough out there, huh?" Chad inquired sympathetically. I gave him a 'pity me' look. Spotting an empty bar stool, I made my way over to it. I hoisted myself up and slid my glass forward. Putting my head down on my folded arms, I let out an audible sigh. Chad laughed, shaking his head. "It'll be all right, Sug."

"Sure, it'll be all right, when I get home, get into my pj's," I grumbled internally. My thoughts were interrupted by the sensation of someone standing behind me. I lifted my head and sat up straight. His voice blasted through me once again. "You're in my seat." I turned my head slightly to the left, glancing over my shoulder. It was him.

Oh, for crying out loud, please don't freak out again, I begged of myself, in my mind. *Just act normal!* I shrieked at myself. I turned all the way around to face the gentleman.

"This?" I pointed downward at the bar stool I was occupying. "This is your seat?" My eyes were wide, my eyebrows were raised so high they could've touched the Milky-way. I was holding my breath again, awaiting his response. He had to think by that point, our second encounter, that I had some sort of mental delay. Fuck, maybe I did. He made me feel a bit out of sorts. Leaning over me to place his empty glass on the bar, he nodded his approval for another gin and tonic to Chad. His chest was touching my arm. His fucking chest…was touching my fucking arm. And, here we go again: I resigned to allow my senses to run amuck. This man's gorgeous dark brown eyes seared my retinas.

"Well," I said seductively; "I suppose I am just going to have to sit on your lap," I continued. He stepped back, smiling, and waved a hand to guide me out of the chair and onto his lap.

Mmm, his lap…

His strong hands curled around my hips as I slid onto his thighs, holding me securely in place. I wrapped my arms around this tall gentleman's neck. Mr. Tall, Dark, and Handsome leaned his amazing jawline toward my face. Feeling his breath on my skin and his voice in my ear made my hormones rage. "My name is Lucas," he said loudly. I leaned my face into his so that we were cheek to cheek, and also so my lips could brush his ear ever so slightly as I spoke.

"My name is, Amber."

I backed my face away from his and held my hand out for him to shake formally. He eyed my hand, amused. Placing his hand in mine and squeezing firmly, he repeated my name, "Amber," he mouthed. He pulled my face closer to his, "Amber, what are you doing working in a place like this, and for a guy like Richard Ward?"

Lucas nodded toward the pool table where Richard Ward, the bar owner, and guys from his pool league were gathered, drinking beers and laughing. One saw him looking and raised his beer. Lucas smiled a dashing smile and raised his glass in return. He grew somber and looked back to me, awaiting my response. Not really wanting to go into the entire story of how it came to be that I was a cocktail waitress, I stammered, "I-well... It's-It's just a job for now. I'm twenty-one, recently divorced, and this is just something until I can do better for myself. I am just kinda feeling my way through life at this point, ya know?"

He smiled at me again, nodding. Lucas leaned in, putting his hand on the small of my back. I leaned in as well. "I am looking for a secretary. I think mine is stealing from me. How about you have lunch with me tomorrow? Here is my card." I took his card and turned it over in my hand, examining it.

Sure-Clean Inc.
Disaster Restoration Services
Lucas Henderson-Owner

I tucked it into my back pocket. "I use my mom's car because I don't have a vehicle yet," I yelled into his ear.

"That's okay, I will come pick you up, write down your information. 10:00 A.M," he continued. I looked into his eyes, smiled, and wrote down my address and cell phone number on a sticky note from the bar. He took the paper, folded it once, and put it in his dress shirt pocket.

Patting my rear-end, Lucas smiled and said, "You should get back to work. Those drinks won't serve themselves. And I should get back to the boys. Tomorrow?" he patted his pocket.

I hopped down, smiling and nodding, "Tomorrow," I repeated, waving goodbye sheepishly. The last couple hours of my shift flew by. Two AM came, I turned in my bank, cashed out, cleaned up, and scooted out of there. Climbing into bed, exhausted but intrigued, I drifted off to sleep with thoughts of Lucas' brown eyes and sideways smile in my head.

* * *

The next morning, Lucas picked me up as scheduled. I sat across from him at a Mexican Restaurant I assumed he frequented due to his rapport with the wait staff. Lucas ordered my meal, my beverage, his meal, and "*Una Cerveza, Por Favor,*" he said, flawlessly.

"So, tell me about you, now that we are in a fairly quiet setting," he inquired. As much as I wanted to be his secretary, I knew I did not have the professional experience. I was still hoping for the best, so I opened up some to him.

"This job would be a game changer for my life situation because I am recently divorced. I worked at Wendy's before I went to work for Richard. I am twenty-one years old, willing to work hard, learn everything I can and apply it, and I am very prompt–always. It is kinda my thing. I-I don't like to be late for anything. Being late makes me feel agitated and behind all day. S-so, I like to be early." I nodded, indicating I was done rambling.

Lucas had an amused smile on his face; that made me even more nervous. Everything about him made me nervous. I couldn't tell what he was thinking. His eyes burned into mine. Sitting back, I cleared my throat, and broke eye contact to look down at my hands. With his left hand, he placed his first two fingers and his thumb around his beer and brought it to his lips, sitting back as well, but never taking his eyes off mine.

I made a mental note, "He is a lefty."

"No, tell me about you. I want to know everything," Lucas pressed.

"Um… Well, like I said, I am divorced and… I-I am goal oriented.

6

I like Japanese food. I like to read," I spewed an onslaught of small truths about myself. Lucas never once took his eyes off me. They drifted down to my lips, which made me hyper-aware of them, my collar bone, the side of my neck, back up to my eyes, my hair, and then back to my eyes.

The food arrived, *Thank god...* I screamed in my head. I breathed a sigh of relief and Lucas looked up from His plate of Chiles Rellenos. "Hungry?" he inquired. *Fuck, he heard me.* I freaked inside, smiling sheepishly and nodding. He smiled a half-smile back and we both began eating.

"So, about your secretary," I began. Lucas sat back, drinking some more of his beer.

"You said she was stealing from you?" Lucas nodded. "How long has she been working for you? I-I mean not that it matters, I suppose, how long she has been working for you. It's wrong, either way. But I am just curious," I babbled on; and he let me.

"Five years," he said stoically.

"I'm sorry that's happening. It must be difficult to be put in the position to have to fire her, hire and train someone else," I empathized.

Lucas took another sip of his beer and placed it back on the table. I caught myself looking at his lips as they pressed against the rim of his beverage. They were the most enticing shade of pinky mauve, slightly wet, smooth... My eyes trailed up his face in lackadaisical fashion. *Oh Jesus, he saw me staring! Fuck, fuck, fuck,* I came unhinged inside briefly.

Lucas waved down the waiter and requested the check. As I sat there, mentally beating myself, he asked me if I had enjoyed my meal. "I did, very much so, thank you."

Lucas nodded. "No problem. Are you all set?" he inquired.

"Yes. I am. Thank you," I replied politely. He helped me out of the booth and escorted me to his truck.

We were about five minutes into our drive back to my house when Lucas spoke, "I have a crew working at a motel over on Ocean Avenue. Would you mind if I stopped in to check up on them? It won't take long."

"Not at all. Please do," I replied. Moments later, we pulled into the Tiki Motel. Lucas hopped out of the truck and walked over to a unit, opened the door, poked his head in and backed out, closing the door. He repeated the process again, twice, with another two rooms; he opened the door, poked his head in, only this time, he disappeared for a couple of minutes inside. Lucas reemerged and motioned for me to come inside. I sat rigid in my seat, deliberating for a split second, *Should I, shouldn't I? You are actually considering this? Going inside a motel room with a complete stranger? How is this even a thought in your head, Amber?* I argued with myself silently.

I grabbed my purse and held it in my lap for a few seconds as Lucas disappeared into the unit. "Fuck it," I decided and opened the truck door. The next thing I knew, I was opening the door to motel room #23. A blast of cold air hit my face and the smell of old carpet and wood filled my nostrils. I stepped all of the way into the unit. Immediately, my scanning eyes landed on Lucas' empty shoes sitting side by side, perfectly lined up, in front of the mini refrigerator to my left. My head swiveled to the right, there was an open beer sitting on the bed side table. The lamp was on, casting a dim yellow glow through its dingy shade. There he was, Lucas, half sitting-half lying on the bed, his black socked feet crossed.

My stomach clenched as I realized what was going to happen. And all that there was of me in this moment of realization was a vast expanse of blank canvas, waiting to be born, to be delivered, rife with potential. Lucas patted the bed, summoning me to come sit beside him. I swallowed hard and sat on the end of the bed to the left of his feet. I placed myself on the corner, purse in lap, knees pressed together tight as white knuckles gripping the metal lap bar on a roller coaster.

My spine felt like a two by four. If he had so much as breathed on me, I would have fallen over, stiff and unflinching; unable to move. I was not certain at all of anything in that moment. I stared ahead at the television flickering. I couldn't tell you what was playing that day to save my life. I can only tell you that the television was most definitely on. My spirit was holding its breath and dying to see what happened next. "Put your purse down and come here to me." His voice, it shattered through me like thirty rounds from an AK-47, every fucking time; completely obliterated.

I sat quietly with my hands on my knees, silently begging for him to riddle my everything with every bit of power he had, and it was a lot. I begged of him with all of my energy as I struggled to understand where all this need in me had sprung from.

Unable to identify it, I resigned, took a deep breath, and placed my purse on the floor slowly but gently. My 2x4 spine hoisted me up, and I watched myself crawl up the bed to him. Hovering on my hands and knees beside his rib cage, I kept my eyes lowered, my heart could not bear to make eye contact with him; it was too faint, too weak, his face looking at any part of my body was a fucking earthquake. Looking upon the face of my complete and utter devastation was like watching someone put a gun to your forehead, tug the hammer back and pull the trigger, point blank. The only outcome is death... Do you watch the face and the actions of your demise, or do you squeeze your eyes closed, and just let them take you down? In the pit of my stomach, a small boulder was chiseling itself into my headstone. I just knew it.

Lucas grabbed my chin and made me look at him. He trailed his hand down my neck, softly cupping it in his palm. I raised my chin instinctively to allow him access, never taking my eyes off his. In that moment, he required all of my flying parts to gather around and look up at him from their knees, with shining eyes, awaiting his next breath in my direction, fully present. In that moment, I had become the *Eta Carinae Nebula* and he was the strong and sturdy arm of the Sagittarius galaxy. With every touch, he reached his nimble, capable fingers into my soul, each finger a shooting star on course to set ablaze every creature that dwelt within me; especially the ones I hadn't become aware of yet.

He placed my hand on the bulge in his dress slacks. I was highly aroused from the moment he had grabbed my chin, but now- I was so close to orgasm, I could barely breathe. I had never wanted someone to be inside of me so badly in all of my life. I was so desperate for it I could already feel him inside of me. The need to have his bare chest heaving itself into mine was deep. It was primal; animalistic. And yet, there we were, both of us still fully clothed.

I rubbed up and down his hard shaft while he explored the upper-half of my body with his hands. Grabbing my wrists, Lucas guided me on top of him. He slid down to lie flat on his back, placed my hands one above each of his shoulders, and ran the fingers of one hand underneath my hair, grabbing a handful of my long mane at the nape of my neck. Lucas began kissing me erratically. He busied his other hand holding my hip steadfast while grinding his rock hard cock into the wetness that was now soaking through my jeans. My knees sunk into the bed as he ripped my lips away from his to jerk my head to the side and back, exposing my neck. He held me in place, just staring at me. His lips were somewhat curled back, exposing his teeth, his breathing heavy and labored.

I couldn't bear to look upon the face of my demise; it was too fucking beautiful. So, I squeezed my eyes shut and waited for him to destroy me.

2

Chapter 2

Lucas released me, tossing me off of him. I landed on my side and then bounced onto my back. His six foot solid frame rose and hovered by the bed, unbuttoning and unzipping his black slacks. I lay there on my back, registering the fact that I was still alive and had just been picked up and tossed off of him like I was a feather; and I was not a tiny thing. As the shock began to fade into the grey matter of my brain, I scooted myself up into a sitting position. My hair was completely disheveled; I straightened myself out, so as to make myself presentable for him once again.

He was completely nude in no time; standing there before me like a bronzed god; he looked spectacular. I could tell Lucas wasted no time getting right down to the bones of things. "Come here to me," he held his hand out. It seemed he had gained a bit more composure. His voice was deep and calm. I swung my feet over the side of the bed, slid off my sandals, and stood. "Now." His voice jolted through me and I flinched. Approaching him, my eyes were lowered to his chest; he gently raised my chin so that his lips would meet mine. I closed my eyes and soaked in this luscious moment.

His soft lips pressed hard against mine. His delicious tongue probed my mouth like a deep sea diver discovering my deepest darkest depths. I melted feeling his tongue sliding across mine, tasting his wanton breath, his hands gliding over my body, undressing me until there I stood before him, completely nude myself. In that moment, I was a stranger to myself. I was watching all of these things happen to this girl, this version of myself allowing this man to undress me, to kiss me, to scare me and intrigue me all at the same time.

It was like standing on the railroad tracks watching this train hurdle itself toward you and the you on the tracks is completely okay with the fact that you know that any second now the train is going to turn you into 80/20 ground prime; and there are two versions of yourself. The version of you that is watching all of this happen from the safety of the concrete is screaming, and she wants to run out there and save you from yourself, but you can't hear her screaming because the train is too loud. The lights are too bright, and you couldn't look away even if you wanted to. The version of the girl on the tracks mouths goodbye to her own horrified tear-streaked face standing within the confines of safety. And then, BAM; it happens, that one moment that changes the course of your life forever.

You become the *carnage.*

Lucas backed me into the wall, my head hitting hard. He grabbed my right leg and wrapped it around his hip. I wrapped my arms around his neck and squeezed him tight for stability as he placed himself inside me. We moved and moaned together, him moving in and out of me slow and hard. With every stroke in, my head bumped the wall.

He placed his hand behind my head and buried his face in my neck. "I-I don-Fuck..uh," I attempted to speak. He pressed harder and faster into me.

"Tell me," Lucas taunted me as he moved the hair from my face and out of my mouth.

"Uh...w-we have to-uh..." I moaned as he pushed into me one more time before pulling out, and roughly turning me around to face the wall. My cheek pressed against the cool wall, I took the opportunity before he put himself inside me and was rendered a stuttering unintelligible mess again.

"Way-way-wait..." I pressed my hand on his thigh. He pulled my hair to the side to expose my neck. I opened my mouth and closed my eyes.

Focus, Amber. Focus, fucking fo-oh Jesus, that feels amazing. I wrestled with my will power internally. Turning around to face him, I spoke up, "Lis-listen, okay?" He kissed me hard, devouring my mouth. "Mmm.. Mm-Mm. Mm-nope, Lucas- Lucas, stop, time-out." I held my hands up in front of my face.

"What is it?" he inquired, looking my body up and down, biting his lip and grabbing my ass, pulling me to him so that I felt his desire pressed into my thighs.

I smiled a lusty grin and continued, "Um, doctors said it was slim to none chance that I would be able to get pregnant again after my son was born, but there is always that possibility that I can get pregnant still, so we-we need to use protection. I don't have any," I managed.

"I am fixed, I had the surgery. We have nothing to worry about," Lucas reassured me. Relaxing a bit, I lowered my hands to his chest and allowed my eyes to wander further south. Trailing my fingertips down his perfect chest, then to his perfect abdomen, and on to his perfect cock, he backed away to give me space to slide down to my knees. Picking up on the cue, I took him into my mouth, tasting him, worshiping this holy piece of Nirvana that he carried between his blessed thighs. Lucas swayed, leaning his head back, moaning, he closed his gorgeous brown eyes.

He ran his thick fingers through my hair as I slid my mouth down his shaft. Gathering a handful of my hair, he held my head in place for several seconds, grunting as he let go. I began to gag and wiped my mouth while looking up at him. "Get on the fucking bed," Lucas commanded through gritted teeth. He watched my every move as I stood and walked to the bed. I could feel his eyes scanning my body as I moved across the room. I crawled onto the bed and lay on my back. He approached the foot of the bed and began to stroke his cock while staring at me. It felt awkward and I wasn't sure what to do, so I just smiled at him uncomfortably. Insecurity began to curl itself around my insides. I grew self-conscious. I wasn't sure what I was supposed to be doing. Lucas was so serious, standing in front of me, doing this incredibly private thing that no man had ever done in front of me before. I simply did not know how to react.

In an instant, it was as if my awkwardness suddenly brought out the beast in him; he stopped what he was doing, leaned over, grabbed my ankles, and threw my legs over his arms. As he pushed himself into me, my body tensed, and my back arched off the bed in response to his body connecting with mine. Impact after impact was made, and I closed my eyes, grabbing my hair with one hand, and the sheets with the other. I had to hold on to something to keep myself from floating away or better yet, to keep from flying into the headboard. Lucas made a savage growling noise as I orgasmed over and over again with every thrust forward. He took my legs and crossed them to signal to me that it was time to turn over. I obeyed, flipping over to my stomach, and clutching the covers in preparation for the storm I knew was brewing.

"Hands on the wall, knees on the bed," he commanded. Without question, I crawled up the bed to the headboard. I placed both of my hands on the wall above the headboard and looked over my shoulder, awaiting his next command. He wasted no time reconnecting with my body. Lucas gathered my waist-length red hair into a ponytail in his hand. He wrapped my hair around his hand twice and yanked my head to the side and back so that I was leaning into his chest, my head resting on his shoulder. "Don't take your hands off of that wall. Do you understand?" he growled into my forehead. I nodded as best I could and squeezed my eyes shut again; waiting for him to eviscerate me.

My fingertips were barely touching the wall and I felt panic set in as he held me there. I could feel his cock brushing my ass and it was driving me crazy. I was a myriad of mixed up mashed together feelings of panic, lust, desire, anxiety, intrigue, and suspense. I didn't want to know what would happen if I had stopped touching that wall for any reason. So, I leaned forward causing myself some pain, as Lucas did not budge or give me reprieve to move even just a bit as he held me there, my hair wrapped around his hands.

The only sound for several minutes was our breathing. "Spread your legs more," he barked. I did as he requested. He scooted in closer, placing himself inside of me. *Thank fucking god, yes, yes, yes!* I screamed inside. I could barely breathe because of how far back my head was, how tightly he was gripping my hair, and now he was pushing himself into me with long, hard, slow strokes that hit a spot that felt so good; I teared up. Having his cock inside me was so fucking beautiful and pleasurable; it made me emotional. It was settled, he was a god. He was my god; and I was now his carnage, his beautiful, fucked up, train wreck. I knew it, and he knew it, because my fingertips never left that wall, not even for a second.

3

Chapter 3

Tears streamed down my face and into my ears. They were cooled by the air conditioner, leaving salty vestiges streaking my cheeks. Lucas released me, my head shooting forward. The blood began rushing back into the places it had been deprived of. My fingers slid down the wall and I clutched the headboard. Panicked, I scrambled to regain contact with the wall. Lucas grabbed my arms at my elbows and fell backward, holding onto me. I went down with him.

My legs bent underneath me as I collapsed onto his chest, he was still inside of me. Lucas pushed me upward so that I could regain my balance. Once steady, I leaned forward, digging my nails into his knees, thrusting my hips back and forth. He was deep inside of me, but I wanted him deeper, I wanted to hurt. So, I leaned back on my knees, unfolded my legs from beneath me in a *crab-walk* position on top of this god, rocking my hips up and down as hard as I could.

I slammed my ass down as hard as I could, over and over again until Lucas took his hands from above his head, where he was holding on to the mattress, and put one around my throat, pulling me down onto him. My back was firmly pressed into Lucas' chiseled chest. His other hand wove into the hair on the top of my head. I stopped moving immediately. I allowed my body to rest atop his. He maneuvered my legs in between his and moved himself in and out of me rapidly, pounding and pounding into me. "Fu-uuhhh-uuuhh-uck-ugh," I moaned. My voice was becoming hoarse; maybe it was his hand tightening around my throat, maybe it was from the steady stream of profanity and sounds coming out of me that even I didn't recognize, either way, I didn't mind one bit.

"You're going to make me cum, you fucking bitch; you ready?" Lucas growled.

"Yes," I whispered, as he violently pushed into me. His hand tightened again around my throat. It became hard for me to breathe in an alarming way. My left hand flew up, grabbing his hand. I was gasping for air. Lucas continued to pound into me. I felt blood rushing into my face, my temples began to throb, my eyes felt like they were bulging in their sockets. I gasped again, as he pushed forcefully into me. I felt a rush of pleasure and panic with every stroke. I started seeing bursts of color, and my eyes began to water. I knew I was in danger of losing consciousness, but I couldn't bring myself to tap his hand, signaling for him to stop. I couldn't make a sound. I could only hold my breath as he plunged into me.

I was terrified, until I realized I hadn't passed out yet. It dawned on me that Lucas was keeping me on the cusp of losing consciousness. It was then that I realized I could continue. He instinctively knew that I was made of far tougher stuff than even I had realized. I let my hand drift from his hand and up into his hair. *Mm, his hair,* I purred to myself. It was so soft, and brown dusted with strands of grey. The smell of his cologne drifted up and filled my nostrils. I breathed in as deeply as I could and began to choke as he pushed into me, so Lucas loosened his grip.

I writhed all over him as his fingers found their way from my throat to my clit. "Fuck, Oh-My-god..." I cried. I released his hair and put both of my hands on top of his hand down there. I stretched and gripping it, the pleasure was intense; it was almost too much-almost... Lucas released my hair and grabbed both of my hands, pulling them away. He raised my hands over his right shoulder with one hand. His other hand held my left hip securely to him. I began to roll to the right as he bucked his hips into me forcefully.

Lucas came out of me and quickly placed himself back inside. He slammed into me one more time and paused, still inside of me. He held himself there firmly, and let my hands go. His hands wandered my body, up and down, grabbing my ass, my hips, over my abdomen and down to my clit, back up, over my rib cage, and to my breasts. Lucas squeezed my breasts possessively. It was slightly painful until he began to move in and out of me again, this time, it was slow and easy. My body ached for him to plow into me as he had been before. I wanted his orgasm terribly, so I made motions with my hips to signal that I wanted him to fuck me harder and faster.

I had never been taken like this before in my life and I needed desperately for it to continue. I needed to feel the panic of struggling to breathe, to hurt, to burn, to ache; I needed it. And he refused me, denied me access to his fucking raging animalistic wild. Instead, his hands slithered and snaked down my body until they found my clit again. He slowly pushed into me upon contact with my little bud. My hands shot down to restrain his, in efforts to keep control of the intense sensations. I couldn't handle being penetrated and having my pussy rubbed at the same time. It was a sensory overload.

"Don't fucking touch me," Lucas snarled.

"I-I-..." I attempted to speak. "I'm sorry," I breathed into his ear. I held my hands out, inches from his. He pushed himself deep into me and pulled out. Opening my hole with one hand, he circled my clit with the other. My hands tangled themselves in my hair. I was ready to receive him again; he placed himself at my entrance and remained just outside, refusing to come inside. I felt a desperation and began to beg. "Please," I heard myself say. I bucked my hips, trying to force him to come inside. "I need you to be inside me, please," I whined, rubbing my body against his.

Lucas stopped rubbing my clit and placed his fingers inside my mouth. "Taste yourself; tell me how you taste..."

I sucked his fingers clean and began to speak, "Kind of sweet, a little salty." I replied.

"Good girl," he replied softly and placed himself inside me again, filling me. I moaned as I felt him slide in. "Do you like the way you taste, Amber?" Lucas inquired. My back arched, and I pressed my head against the mattress for leverage. The upper half of my body was sliding off his. He held me in place, his fingers still in my mouth. "Answer me," Lucas demanded.

"Yes," I moaned. He began pushing into me slowly but firmly.

"Yes, Sir," Lucas commanded me to self-correct and stopped fucking me. He paused, his cock deep inside of me, waiting for my response.

"Yes, Sir," I replied.

My head was hanging off the bed, my hands were in my hair, mouth open, and I was feeling slightly dizzy when Lucas grabbed my waist, pulling me back onto the bed. "Get on your back." I did as I was told. He placed himself between my thighs and pushed into the place that made me call upon god. I could feel every muscle in his abdomen twitching and contracting. He buried his face into my neck and hair. He laced his fingers together around the top of my head, wrapping me up in a cocoon. My legs wound themselves around the back of his thighs, desperately trying to pull him as far into me as I could. I needed him to bruise me in a soul deep way so that I would feel his presence in me for a week after we had parted ways. And he made me believe that it was possible. Lucas was quickly becoming my salvation. He began fucking me with such fury and conviction that my soul had started waving her white flag and army crawling out of my mouth. He delivered me from the very core of my wretched existence. He opened the cage door. *Lucas, You are terrifying, and strange, and beautiful,* my heart sang as he blew my insides apart.

My eyes rolled into my head somewhere. He was plugged in and the connection was sound. Our electricity was flowing and arching. He plunged deep into me, holding me in place so that every drop of his fluids drained into me. Lucas moaned, "Fuck, I'm cumming, I'm cumming," loudly as my nails dug into his shoulder blades and raked down his back. He slammed into me three more times, groaning with each thrust. I closed my eyes and held on to his lower back. I held him in place an extra few seconds, I wanted to feel him spraying into my folds and recesses. Lucas collapsed, spent, into my arms. I lightly stroked his back and released him from the grip of my thighs. We lay there together, his cock twitching inside of me.

4

Chapter 4

There was a distant ringing in my ears, it's the ringing you hear in the presence of absolute and utter silence. My brain was compensating for the severe lack of thought and noise inside. It wasn't used to complete silence and peace. I had a beautiful man atop me, trembling still as he pulled out, and it blew my mind.

"Hi," Lucas said to me breathlessly, brushing my sweat drenched hair from my face before kissing me.

"Hi," I smiled into his kiss. I pressed my lips together, tasting his kiss as he maneuvered his way off the bed.

"Need some water?" Lucas retrieved two bottles from the refrigerator, handing me one. I nodded, sitting up. We both looked at each other while drinking them down. The air conditioner was blowing a clump of very knotted hair on the side of my head back and forth. I continued to drink and did my best to straighten it out.

Lucas kissed my forehead and headed into the bathroom. I heard him peeing, the toilet flushed, and the shower turned on. *I am guessing this means, get my clothes on*, I thought to myself. I fell back, allowing my head to hit the mattress with a thud. "god, I don't want to move," I smiled. I let my body relax, and as I did so, I felt him draining out of me. I looked for something to wipe myself up with and found nothing. So, I lay there wondering if I should use the sheet or just dress and clean up before we left.

I opted to dress and tidy up to the best of my ability once Lucas was finished. The shower turned off just as I was sliding my right foot into my sandal. I had managed to find all articles of my clothing, which was pleasantly surprising considering the fashion in which they were removed from my body and flung as if they were villains attacking and invading his castle. Lucas stepped out of the bathroom, towel around his waist. I looked up and smiled. "It's all yours," he stepped aside allowing me to enter, and kissing me deeply before I passed by.

He smelled like ivory soap.

I closed the door and cleaned myself up. I was a wreck, and better yet, I had a viscous knot of matted hair on the side of my head, the likes of which I had never seen. Combing through it with my fingers to no avail, I decided to just pull my hair up into a messy bun. Situation handled... I sat down to pee and saw the tiny square of soap sitting on the side of the tub. Running my fingers over its tacky surface, a sideways smile formed. *His body is incredible*, I bit my lip. I exited the bathroom to find Lucas finishing his beer. "You ready?" he inquired.

"I am," I replied. He showed me to the door and followed me out.

The ride home was a quiet one. We didn't make eye contact. His phone ringing made me jump. It was the classic Nokia tone, high-pitched and melodic. "Sure-Clean, this is Lucas," he answered. I continued to stare straight ahead. "Yes. I told the homeowner we would have two guys in there to finish the job by 3:00 P.M. Then what is his issue?" Lucas raised his voice. "Just... Do what you can to make him happy. I'll be over that way in the next thirty minutes..." He hung up. "god damn it; some of these fucking home owners act like I have no other clients besides them," Lucas vented.

I released the death grip I had on my purse strap and touched his thigh. He looked over at me and smiled. "I'm sorry you had to hear that, he apologized.

"No, it's okay. I understand that you have a business to run. It seems very stressful." I sympathized.

Lucas sighed, "It has its moments. Especially, when you have a bunch of dumb-asses working for you and impossible clients." I squeezed his thigh. He looked over and smiled at me. My heart raced, and my pussy throbbed again. *Oh, for Pete's sake, Amber...* I scolded myself.

We turned onto Blackmore Blvd. Traffic was merging here from the highway heading South. We sat at the stop light quietly, watching the cars. Sadness was becoming a bowling ball in my stomach. I was only about five minutes from home. I didn't want to go home after having such a magnificent experience with this god. "See right down there?" Lucas pointed toward a side street with a set of railroad tracks that crossed it.

"Uh huh," I replied, looking in the direction of his finger.

"My office is right down there, in Gellar Plaza," he continued.

"Oh! Okay," I replied. "How long have you owned Sure-Clean?" I inquired.

"Twelve years now. I built it from the ground up," Lucas stated proudly.

"That is impressive. I respect that a lot," I replied.

The light turned green. And moments later, we were turning into my neighborhood.

He put the truck in park on the curb outside my house. We sat in silence for a moment. Lucas looked at his hands solemnly. The stress on his face worried me. That look on a man's face is never good news, he was going to tell me he never wanted to see me again. That or he needed me to make a quick exit, so he could make his, so that we just go on with our lives, because this was strictly a lightning strike kind of deal; and perhaps, he was wanting to move along like storms do, and strike in other people's Universes. I had that heart in my throat, stomach full of boulders, feeling.

Lucas cleared his throat. *Go ahead and smite me*, I thought to myself. "I need to tell you something," he said, his tone grave. *Here we go; how embarrassing*, I replied in my head.

"Oh-okay?" I stumbled. Another moment of silence ensued...

"I am-married..." Lucas looked up and stared straight ahead, his

23

jaw tight, face stern, unblinking. He swallowed hard, waiting for my response. My eyes widened as I attempted to choke down this statement. I looked at him refusing to look at me.

Married, married, married, married, this word bounced off the Gyri and Sulci of my brain. The news refused to slow itself enough to be absorbed, so it just ping ponged about until I found a reply.

"I-should uh," I pointed to my house.

"Go," he finished my sentence. A sentence it was. *Go, go, go, go*, another word hurling itself against the interior of my skull. I reached for the door handle, fumbled, and managed to get it open. The truck door swung itself wide open with a slight bounce back. It was as if the Universe was smiling smugly down upon me saying, *Don't let the door hit you on your way out, homewrecker.*

I felt a hand on the back of my arm. I stopped mid-movement and looked down and to the side to see Lucas looking at me. The pain evident in his eyes, he said softly, " But I need to see you again. Can I-see you again?" I slid back into the seat, putting my legs into the truck. I sat there looking down at the floor. Lucas grabbed my chin and made me look at him. His eyes drifted from mine to my mouth. He stared at my mouth, and I stared at his eyes staring at my mouth. I closed my eyes instinctively as he pulled my face to his.

He pressed his lips to mine. I could feel his need, his desire to have me again. I wanted him to have me, to claim me. He pulled away and sat back, his head leaning against the headrest. "You should probably go. They are going to worry about you." He spoke softly, referring to my mother and her boyfriend. I grabbed my purse again and nodded. "I'll call you?" Lucas inquired.

"I'd like that a lot," I replied. We looked at one another.

"Think about it, Amber," Lucas urged. I nodded again.

"I will," I replied and got out of the truck.

5

Chapter 5

He sat there until I had made it inside. The sound of his diesel rumbling out of the neighborhood brought on a sense of sadness and relief. I mumbled a quick greeting to my mother and her boyfriend on the way to my room. My bed-It was a beautiful sight. I walked over and fell face first into it. My body making impact made a satisfying 'poof' sound. I lay there, morbidly still, attempting to capture, and hold captive, one singular thought. Everything was still ping ponging around in my head. Unsuccessful, I rolled over onto my back and lay there, breathing deeply to calm my body, in hopes that my mind would shortly follow.

Fucking married; I should've known. Men that handsome and incredible in bed are never single. I was raised with better values than the behavior I exhibited today. I just had sex with a married man. I had sex with a stranger, who is a married man, in a grimy motel room that smelled like mold, mildew, and rotting carpet. This is a new low for you, Amber. What-the-FUCK! I mentally berated myself, and put my pillow over my eyes and forehead, holding it there tightly. But there was no escaping the movie and script my mind was playing on loop behind my eyelids.

Oh, but it gets better! No, Amber... You don't immediately exit the vehicle AS YOU SHOULD HAVE! You let him kiss you and suck you back in with-with his... his fucking delicious mouth. Fuck me... it was incredible. I felt the anger begin to fade into a subtle pulsing down there. My thoughts diverted. My pussy felt really, really amazing. I bit my lip, remembering the part where he did *that thing* with his fingers on my bits..."*Don't fucking touch me,*" Lucas' voice rang out in my head. My hands hovering above his by only inches, him as far inside of me as he could possibly be, being full of him, so very, very-full of him. god, his cock was outstanding. The hormones this man had triggered were spurting their chemicals into my veins like blood from a punctured jugular. They were seeping into my system, making a complete and utterly distasteful, reckless, monster out of me.

Shower, cold shower, frostbite-cold shower...NOW! I screamed at myself inside. I took the pillow from over my eyes and leapt from the bed, gathered my clothes, and headed for the bathroom. I turned on only the cold water, undressed, and stepped in as far from the spray as possible. "Fuckkkk, c-coldddd. Sh-shit... Fuck this." I turned the hot water on to a comfortable temperature. I stood in the spray for several moments without a thought in my head as my body regulated and began to relax. It felt good to wash the sweat off. After I washed my hair and body, I turned the water to a heat that was a bit beyond my comfort level and let it sear my skin. The pain felt good. It made me feel extra clean, and that, I desperately needed to feel.

I got out and air dried as I conditioned and combed through my severely knotted hair. My scalp was sore. I wiped a section of the steamed mirror clear and checked myself for visible marks. There were none. I was somewhat disappointed. I dressed and lay down for a nap for a few hours before work. Getting to sleep was easier than I had anticipated. I awoke with a start three hours later and knocked my alarm clock radio off my nightstand trying to turn off Britney Spears blaring from its speakers. Scrambling to pick it up off the floor, I knocked it under my bed further. I rolled off my bed and onto the floor, swiping at the radio until I made contact. I snatched it, holding it to my chest, it silenced itself. Sitting there on my knees, clutching the radio to my chest, my heart raced obnoxiously. I placed it back on my nightstand and prepared myself for work. "I'm headed out,

Momma. I'll see y'all later- love you," I yelled on my way out the door.

"Love you too! Be careful," she called as the door closed.

* * *

My Saturday shift came and went uneventfully. The week following was chaotic and exceptionally busy as I had picked up extra shifts from a few servers going on vacation together. I didn't give much thought to my conversation with Lucas until Friday morning rolled around. My boss called me to thank me for covering everyone's shifts and to tell me to take the weekend off.

"Wow! Thank you, Richard!" I gushed.

"Hey, no problem, darlin'. Enjoy your weekend!" he replied.

I tossed my phone on the bed and flopped down. "A whole weekend; no work, absolutely nothing to do..." I smiled. "This is nice." I fell backward, allowing my arms to flop above my head.

My phone buzzed; a text message from a number I didn't recognize.

I need to see you.

My heart slowed down and sped up all at the same time. It was him. I could feel his energy swirling around me through the phone. I could smell his cologne and his sweat.

Another message came through.

Lucas:
Amber, come to me tonight.

All of my flying parts scattered like crystalline shards of mirror. I saved his number into my phone and began smiling like a fool. I rolled my eyes and shook my head at how a text from him made me feel so—so much of everything all at once.

I responded.

Amber:
What time and where?

Seconds later, my phone buzzed again in my hands.

Lucas:
8:00 P.M, my boat–Anchors Away–Blue Heron Marina, on the north side. Are you familiar with it?
Amber:
I have never been there. I've passed by it, though. What is the address, just in case?
Lucas:
1742 Blue Heron Way. My boat is the fourth slip down on the left, first dock. Call me if you have any issues finding it and I will meet you out there.
Amber:
I will be there.

My phone went silent; the conversation was over, just like that. I had plans, I had a date; a date with a married man, to have sex. This was a bomb, sure to explode and have dire consequences. But this man said things to me like, I need to see you again, can I see you again, come to me, and he fucked me like no other. In order to make myself okay with what I was about to do, I began to rationalize and justify my choice. My logic was that his wife apparently wasn't meeting his needs and so he has come to me, and we have this once in a lifetime kind of chemistry; my body, when he touched it, melted. Pacing my room, I felt a surge of power run through me.

"Fuck it. I am not feeling bad. I am single. I am not doing anything wrong. What he does is his and his wife's issue to deal with, not mine. What she refuses to do at home, I will gladly handle."

I got ready, extra-extra sexy, a spritz of jasmine and orange perfume strategically placed, hair cascading perfectly down my back, multiple necklaces of different lengths swung from my neck, a black form-fitting low-cut shirt clung to all the right places. Donning a pair of light wash exceptionally snug jeans and my best pair of strappy black stiletto heels, I got the keys to my mother's Taurus, and headed Lucas' way.

I texted him.

Amber:
On my way now.

Lucas:
See you when you get here, drive carefully.

It was dusk when I arrived. I checked the time, it was 7:50 pm. *I'm a bit early. But I am certain he won't mind*, I pondered as I checked my scarlet lips in the rearview mirror. I made my way down the first dock toward the fourth boat on the right, 'Anchors Away' was Lucas' boat's name. "Here we go," I took a deep breath.

Lucas appeared in the door of the cabin below.

"You made it," he smiled.

I smiled back broadly, "I did!"

He gave me his hand, "Here, let me help you. Getting on this thing can be a bit tricky. I'd hate for you to fall."

I took his hand, "Thank you. I appre-OH!"

I stepped onto the boat with a stumble. Falling into Lucas' arms, he caught me around my waist before I completely landed on my bottom.

"Oh my god. I am so embarrassed," I covered my face and laughed uncomfortably, as I pushed off of his chest.

"Are you okay? It looks like you twisted your ankle a bit," he inquired.

My face was now the color of my painted lips.

"I-I am okay. Thank you. I appreciate you catching me."

Lucas smiled his beautiful sideways smile and pointed at my shoes.

"I know! Not the best fashion decision I've ever made."

I laughed a nervous laugh, closed my eyes, and covered my forehead, embarrassed. He ushered me to the bench on my right, and I sat as he had prompted me to. He knelt in front of me and patted his knee. I looked at Lucas, confused. He took my calf and pulled my foot toward him and placed it on his knee. He ran his hands down my denim clad leg and found the gold buckle on my ankle. His fingers maneuvered the delicate contraption with ease and gently tugged my foot free from my high heel. He did the same to my other foot. Lucas stood, extending his hand out toward me. In such a state of shock, I just sat there, aghast, with my left hand over my heart, mouth open, eyes wide. When I realized my mouth was getting a bit dry, I snapped back to reality and took my hand from my heart to take his, allowing him to lead me down into the cabin.

6

Chapter 6

"It's cramped quarters. Watch your head coming down these last two steps," Lucas instructed.

He placed his hand on the ceiling above me as I stepped down into the cabin so as to ensure I did not, indeed, bump my head. I smiled at the gesture and took his outstretched hand.

"Such a gentleman," I teased him with a coy smile.

The queen bed lay before me, made up neatly. A small television to the right, bracketed to the wall, flickered the news, and the sound was muted. The space was small but cozy.

"Do you ever worry about any of your stuff falling off when the boat rocks?" I questioned curiously.

He laughed softly. "The water in the marina is relatively calm unless a boat or something runs through; then there are some waves, but they have mostly dissipated by the time they reach the docks," he responded.

I looked around, taking it all in.

"This is the bathroom, if you need to go. It is so small you have to turn sideways to get in, at-least I do. So, watch yourself in there as well. I plan to get a 42-foot yacht in the near future. But for now, this is my home away from home." Lucas' voice trailed off as his eyes became sad and far away. His gaze met mine as I stood there staring at him, reading him, waiting for him to share more with me.

Noticing that I had picked up on the change in tone and energy, he looked away, avoiding further eye contact.

"I am going to go up and get a beer, want anything? I have soda and water on ice. You can have a beer, if you want. I don't know what kind you drink, but... You can-" He talked as he headed top side.

"Just water for me, thank you," I called up to him.

He came back down several minutes later carrying two beers in one hand and two waters in the other. I took the one he handed to me. He stood in front of me for a moment, looking into my eyes with a very palpable predator/prey energy emanating from him. I stared back and swallowed the growing lump in my throat, unable to move, blink, or breathe.

The silence and chemistry in the small distance between us was so heavy and thick it felt like Macon, Georgia in the dog days of summer. He stepped forward, leaning into me, pressing me backward onto the bed. Lucas sat the other water he had brought down on the window sill to my right. My heart raced, and I sunk into the bed with my eyes closed, and then, nothing happened.

My eyes popped open. I released my vice-like grip on the comforter and lifted my head to find him standing at the foot of the bed looking at me in that predatory way again. I felt my face flush, my ears and cheeks burnt with embarrassment. I straightened my hair, cleared my throat to break the silence and tension in the room, and slid into a sitting position once again. He drank down a long gulp of beer and sized me up. I swallowed hard again as I sat there, hands in lap, feeling awkward and embarrassed at how swept away I had become.

I wasn't quite sure what to do with myself, so I just sat there looking at him looking at me. My eyes traveled his body until I noticed the bulge in his pants. I took a deep breath in and slowly released it, trying to calm myself. Lucas' hand came into view. He began touching himself. I couldn't take my eyes off him. I began to bite my lip as he moved closer to me.

"Take off your shirt," he commanded.

I did as I was told, without hesitation. He squeezed himself and wet his lips with a quick swipe of his pink tongue. I looked into his eyes, awaiting his next command.

Lucas stepped to the end of the bed, unbuttoning his shirt and pulling it off his shoulders. It hit the floor. What a beautiful sound; what a beautiful sight... It was the sight and sound of my undoing, of my ruin. I allowed my eyes to roam his body, admiring his toned abdomen, his perfectly built frame, just the right amount of hair on his chest and down his stomach. I was craving him fiercely.

"Touch them," he said, staring at my 36DD breasts.

I brought my hands to my black lace bra and explored myself while staring into his eyes. Slipping a strap off my left shoulder with my right hand and then the other strap from my right shoulder with my left hand, I tucked my fingers around the sides of my breast, hugging myself.

Lucas unbuttoned and unzipped his pants and they dropped to the floor. I looked at him, longing to be able to just close my eyes, make a wish, and then open them, and he would be inside of me; tearing me apart, my neck exposed to him. I was pleading with him, with every ounce of mental telepathy and body language I had, to take me by the throat and throttle me until the lights went out; until I was on the brink of certain death, and then kiss me back to life. Lucas brought the darkness out in me, and it was a little frightening, but mostly it felt incredible and all encompassing; and I needed more and more.

He was wearing no underwear and in his full glory, he stood naked before me, fully erect, lips curled back into a slightly disturbing but sexy demonic smile; he had some fucking plans for me.

He ran his hand across his chest, spread his stance to slightly over shoulder width apart, and stroked his cock to my body. My pussy was throbbing and shrieking; my everything was pulsing, pounding, pushing, and caving in on itself.

My breaths quickened as my heartrate shot up, my head falling to the left, as I watched him pleasure himself. This was real life; I was in this god's bed, on his boat, topless, and already cumming in my panties, without him ever having touched me. I could feel the cum trickling out of me. My nipples were so hard they were burning. Emboldened, I took my bra the rest of the way off, came out of my jeans, and slid to the end of the bed. I spread my legs and put one on each side of his strong thighs. Placing my hands, palm down, on his stomach, I closed my eyes resting my forehead against him, still as a mouse, trying to hide from the cat. As soon as my hands made contact with the firm but soft warm flesh of his lower abdomen, I was calm, like Zen calm...

I breathed in his scent. Lucas ran the fingers of his left hand through my hair and down to the side of my face. I leaned into his palm that he had cupped around my chin. Pulling my face upward, our eyes met. We maintained that connection for a couple of minutes; his face was tender, and peaceful, and adoring. I was violently yanked from the beauty of the moment when his left hand found the back of my hair and lurched my head backward and to the left. The unexpected shift from tender to violent frightened me and I slid down to my knees before him. My hand shot up to grasp the hand that was gripping my hair, my other hand on his right thigh.

I whimpered and cringed as pain shot through my scalp.

"Open," Lucas commanded. He gripped his cock with his right hand, and forcefully pushed it into my mouth.

"Mmm," I moaned.

The pain became an afterthought with every desperate thrust into my cheeks and throat. Clad only in my soaked panties, forced to kneel before him, force fed his hard cock, and admittedly, I wasn't at all displeased about it. I was finally in sync with his rhythm. Putting my hands on each hip, I greedily took him into my mouth again and again, sucking down his oozing pre-cum. He pinched my nostrils closed with two fingers and slammed into my throat with an extraordinarily hard thrust and held my head in place for several seconds. I felt the blood rushing into my face, my eyes watered, and my gag reflex had kicked in. I began to squirm and dry heave with his cock shoved firmly past my tonsils. I tapped his thigh and he released my head. My upper body shot back, elbows landing on the end of the bed. I sat there catching my breath, pussy throbbing, gagging, mascara running from the tears that were now spilling down my cheeks.

A string of his cum and slobber that had leashed me to his cock, broke free and dripped down between my breasts. I looked at him, feeling nauseated from swallowing down the rather large amount of semen he had released down my throat. I wiped my mouth with the back of my hand, feeling the trail of his cum cooling on my face. I sat on my knees, staring up at him; both of us were panting. He was awaiting my response to his brutality, and I was turned on beyond measure. Never taking my eyes off his, I rose from my knees, turned around, bent over the bed and stretched out my arms to span its length. I placed my face, left cheek down, on the mattress, and closed my eyes, offering my body to him to use as he pleased.

Lucas pulled my panties to the side and plunged into me. He let out a primal grunt/growl. god, I loved when he made that sound. I didn't care who heard, I screamed and howled, my eyes rolled into the back of my head as he grabbed my elbows, yanking me about like a rag doll tearing into his prey with the ferocity of a famished lion.

Use me, my god; my body is yours, I said to him secretly.

7

Chapter 7

"Get all the way onto the bed," Lucas demanded and pushed into me hard one last time.

He slapped my ass with a loud 'thwack'. My head shot up, surprised by the impact. The mess that was my mop of unruly red hair whipped down my back.

"Umph," I grunted involuntarily.

I froze momentarily, allowing the stinging on my bottom to translate. I observed that the pain felt good. It heightened my awareness to the pulsing in my pussy. It centered me enough to really focus on what was happening in my body.

Crawling up the bed after me, Lucas grabbed the soaked crotch of my panties. They slid over my hips and halfway down my thighs. I twisted around, flopping down on my back. I giggled at him. He smiled a playful sideways smile and crawled up the bed toward me, pulling my panties the rest of the way off, and tossing them somewhere. Slowly, he pressed his body down on top of me, devouring my mouth with his.

His cock pressed into my thighs, leaving trails of cooling semen wherever it touched. Lucas was dripping for me, just as much as I was for him. It turned me on that his body responded to mine in the ways that it did, that he made it so evident, his desire for me. He wrapped his arms over the top of my head, tangling his fingers in my hair, just like last time. Cocooning me, he pressed himself into me, ever so slowly sliding in.

His abdomen trembled, and he let out the sexiest moan. My thighs and pussy tightened in response.

"You're so fucking tight," he breathed into my ear.

I leaned my head into his face. Lucas kissed my collarbone. I nudged his face away and began kissing his neck. I wanted him to pound and pour into me like the savage that he had shown me he can be. I needed him to scare me, hurt me, wound me... He continued to caress me and grip my thighs lustfully. I felt myself growing irritated that he was being so tender with me and not giving me what I wanted, so, I bit him, and I bit him hard.

The first bite was semi-hard in that luscious space between his shoulder and neck; the second, his jaw line. I clamped down and swiveled my hips, attempting to force him to fuck me harder. Lucas lifted himself from me, sat upright, and grabbed my throat, pulling me up on top of him. My legs slid over his hips.

"Yes," I garbled.

Holding my throat tighter than he ever had, he pushed into me forcefully. Using the leverage he had by choking me, he pushed my body hard and fast down onto his cock.

I wrapped my arms around his head and held him tightly to my chest. He let go of my throat and grabbed two handfuls of my ass and spread me open. I ran my hands through his hair as I pushed down on him with every ounce of energy I had. My head fell back, and I rocked and swayed on top of my god. Silvery wisps of moonlight began to shine through the small windows in the cabin. I howled, cried, moaned, and screamed until I had almost no voice left.

"Get on your knees; I want to see that beautiful ass in the air," Lucas said gruffly.

I did as he requested. Playfully, I swished my hips side to side, enticing him to hurry up and get resituated. I grabbed a sip of water while he drank down the rest of his beer. He climbed back into the bed and placed himself to be inside of me again.

"Would-um," I began. "I was just wondering, I mean, if you would um… push-like, push my head into the pillow, while we…" I looked over my shoulder to gauge his response.

"If you'd like me to," he said softly.

"I mean, hard," I emphasized.

He smiled and nodded, running his hands over my pale freckled skin, glowing in the moonlight.

"No, I mean… like, really hard. I mean, like… I don't want to be able to breathe. I want to be-afraid of you," I reemphasized, feeling completely awkward yet turned on by the feeling of his strong hands roaming and worshiping my body.

He said nothing. I remained silent and still.

He slid his left hand over the small of my back with the tenderness of centuries old lovers. He traveled up to my shoulder blades and gently pushed my chest down onto the bed. He placed himself inside of me; sliding in slowly, Lucas pressed his cock as deeply into my recesses as he could and trembled. I smeared my face into the pillow, rubbing it like a cat in heat. That tremble… It practically made me orgasm every fucking time. He held me in place. The grip he had on my hips hurt so incredibly good. I could feel pressure from him in my lower abdomen, the way he had positioned me.

"Oh my god," I moaned, my fingers feeding the pillow into my mouth.

Lucas pulled out sharply and paused. I could feel air rush into me. I was wide open for him, ready to receive him again, and again, and again.

"Please, please come back," I begged, whispering to him.

He leaned forward and gathered my hair, gently pulling it into a low ponytail. He wrapped it around his left hand twice and shifted onto his feet into a squatting position over me. And then, he did it; he plowed into me. My head lurched back, and I scrambled to find something to grip, something to hold onto for dear life. Lucas pushed into me forcefully, savagely. Letting go of my hair, he pushed my face into the pillow. He moved in and out of me in rapid succession, fucking me furiously; not one ounce of mercy...

I was struggling to breathe but refused to tap or signal that I needed him to relent. My state of mind was drifting somewhere between ultimate pleasure and bliss to frightened to feeling 'floaty' and out of body. It-was-incredible. He let up ever so slightly, and I turned my head, so I could get a bit of air. I breathed a few good breaths and he snatched the pillow from beneath me, placing it over my head. Lucas resumed fucking me. I found an air pocket where the pillow bent over the side of my face and breathed as shallow as possible. I refused to give up, to signal for help.

I don't tap out, I reminded myself through muffled moans and cries.

He took the pillow off my head and turned me onto my back. Wiping the hair from my face and mouth, he pressed his lips to mine. Cocooning me with my arms held down above my head, he pushed into me again, slowly. I felt the length of him massaging those places that made me call on God and mutter unintelligible things, and the tears came. This man... This god... This heathen... Us two... How fucking beautiful.

"Fuck... I'm-I'm gonna..." Lucas moaned.

"Yes, please," I urged, craving to feel him throb and release into me.

He buried his face into my neck and pressed into me half and quarter strokes, moaning, panting, and pouring his cum into me. I held him there until I was sure he had fully released. I wanted it all. He kissed me and rolled over onto his back, spent. We lay there panting, our hands on our hearts. We glanced at one another, shared a laughed, and stared at the ceiling, trying to slow our heart rates.

8

Chapter 8

I took in a deep breath and let out an audible sigh. Lucas nodded in agreement.

"You are incredible," I said, smiling and rolling over to face him.

I placed my hand on his chest.

"As are you, my dear."

He placed his hand on top of mine and we lay there for a few moments in silence with our eyes closed, enjoying the cold air settling over our sweat drenched bodies and faces.

"I am going to grab a beer. Do you want anything?"

Lucas patted my thigh, signaling me to move so he could get up.

"No, thank you; I still have a little water left," I replied.

He slid down to the end of the bed and headed toward the bathroom. I lay there in the chaos of bunched covers and the frenzy of pillows thrown about, smiling. I licked my parched lips and begrudgingly shifted into a sitting position to grab my bottle of water.

I looked at my phone to check the time as I chugged down my water. Lucas appeared in the narrow stairway, ducking the overhang as he took the last few steps down. I smiled and brushed my hair back from my face.

"Someone calling?" He nodded toward the phone in my hand.

I looked down at my phone and then back at him. "Oh no, I was just checking the time. It's getting pretty late; I should get going," I replied.

I finished my water in the silence, under Lucas' indeterminate gaze. Scooting to the edge of the bed, I stood and lost my balance once again, falling into his strong arms.

"Apparently, I can no longer walk, thanks for that," I quipped; we both laughed.

I placed my hand on his chest and looked up at him adoringly before breaking away to slip into the bathroom. He was on the upper deck when I came up the stairs. Feet firmly on the top deck, I found him bent over the cooler, digging in the mostly melted ice slush.

I wrapped my arms around him from behind. Lucas stood upright, holding my arms securely around his waist. He turned his head to the left, looking over his shoulder at me. Eyes closed, my face was buried between his shoulder blades, reveling in the sensation of his cool tacky skin against my cheek. We stood still for a few moments in silence. Patting my hands, he signaled for me to release him. I complied, and he turned to face me, putting both hands on my face, one on each cheek. Lucas looked into my eyes, scanning my features intently. His deep brown eyes traveled my cheekbones, my jawline, my lips, my nose, and back down to my lips, where he settled, staring lustfully.

He began to sway slightly, and I followed suit. His breathing grew quietly rapid, his shoulders became squared and rigid. I bit my lip, as the sweet, innocent moment quickly had drained into the gutter. I let slip a soft moan as he devoured my mouth, bending me backward. Lucas pulled away, his gaze turning dark and lusty.

He stood me upright, saying, "You should go now before your ass is bent over my bed again."

I knew he meant every word, so I straightened my hair and clothes, and slid around him to grab my shoes.

"I will just put these on in the car."

I stepped forward to exit the boat and Lucas grabbed my arm.

"No, you won't. You will put them on here. You could step on a hook out there. We are at a Marina, you know?"

I paused, my eyes traveling from his face to his hand firmly gripping my arm, and then back to his face. Without question, I sat and put my heels on. He stepped off the boat and extended his hand to me. I took it and allowed him to guide me off the boat until both feet were steadily planted on the dock.

"You good?" he asked, slightly amused.

I laughed, playfully pushing his chest. He grabbed my wrist, holding it to his chest. The smile faded from my mouth. His stare burned into my soul, shriveling every ounce of comfort in a microsecond.

"I want to see you again."

His eyes flashed the same intensity they had when he told me he was married. I looked at his hand gripping my wrist and my pussy clenched.

He let go and placed his hand softly against my face, his thumb stroking my lips and cheek. A breeze blew some strands of hair over my forehead and nose, tickling my skin, the heat from his hand, the silk blanket of sea air licking my goosebumps, lightning muted by thick cloud cover and moonlight flickering over the waterway... It was a magical evening. I wrapped an arm around myself and tucked my fluttering hair behind my ear, looking down.

"I do need to see you again," nodding my agreement.

My eyes found his, searching for approval. The way he had tilted his head, his eyes were sparkling as they caught the moonlight. Lucas pulled me to him and kissed my forehead. I closed my eyes and wrapped my arms loosely around his waist, running my hands down the contour of his back.

Breaking away, I said, "I should-" and motioned toward my mother's Taurus station wagon in the parking lot.

"Go," he finished my sentence.

"Yeah. I should... I need to," I replied and stepped away, walking backward six or seven steps, unable to take my eyes off him.

I begrudgingly turned and walked with firm resolve to the car. *No turning back, no regrets*, I mumbled a reminder to myself. I glanced in the rearview mirror as my taillights lit up the entrance to the dock.

Empty. No more him. Gone, just like that. Our time was done and that meant back to my reality, my world, to try to pretend I was just a normal twenty-one-year-old getting her life together. That dock represented a gateway to Heaven and Hell now. Praise it being the bridge to my god; curse it being the sentence to my entrance back into a world that would never fucking understand me.

9

Chapter 9

The drive home happened; simple as that. I don't recall much of it as my mind and sated body were cocooned in a sleepy, happy, magical land far-far away. The key to my front door hit the lock, and the next thing I knew, I was sitting on my bed, tugging my heels off. Next, was the shower, where I leaned against the cool wall, breathing in the steam from the hot water. And finally, I was in bed, lying still as the dead, with my unusually steady hands folded over my abdomen. I relived that evenings events, a highlight reel that had nestled itself inside of my head—it was comforting. It was like being tightly swaddled and cradled in loving arms. I drifted off into the most peaceful sleep I had ever experienced.

The sound of birds chirping and a blinding ray of sunlight that burned through my eyelids woke me abruptly. I was still lying in the same position I had fallen asleep in. *Impressive*, I thought. I checked my phone—nothing from Lucas. I dropped it onto the bed and put my hand over my eyes, assessing how I was feeling. Nothing... I felt Zero-Zilch-Nada; my constantly swirling thoughts had found themselves silenced. It was the vacuum of space in my head and in my heart. Anxiety began rearing its head.

"I'm literally freaking out because I am not freaking out right now," I admonished myself.

I laughed out loud for being so ridiculous and swung my legs over the side of my bed. The rest of my body followed, making my way to the coffee pot. Hovering over the percolating coffee maker, I crossed my arms, smiling and squeezing myself as I breathed in the delicious bold roast scent.

I floated through three days of no stress, no anxiety, no spinning, spiraling thoughts that I couldn't control. I felt more peace and focus than I had ever felt in my lifetime. By the end of day three, I could sense the calm I had experienced the first couple of days after mine and Lucas' evening together melting into a strange sadness. I couldn't quite put my finger on why, but it was there and had quickly begun to replace the happiness. I got the feeling that something was missing but couldn't identify what it was. So, I decided to reach out to Lucas.

Amber: *Hey.*

Moments later…

Lucas: *Hey there. What are you doing?*

Amber: *Thinking about you.*

Lucas: *Oh yeah?*

Amber: *Yeah. :)*

Lucas: *I am at the office. You close by?*

I smiled at my phone.

Me: *I am.*

Lucas: *See you in 10?*

My heart began to race. My smile was so wide it made my face hurt. I sat up abruptly and responded.

Me: *5*

I dressed quickly, calling out to my mom as I grabbed the car keys to let her know I was heading out for a bit. The sadness I felt had vanished the moment I heard from him. The prospect of seeing him filled the void. It perplexed me how I could leap from such severely varied degrees of emotion in seconds. And nothing was the same anymore. It was all a little upside down. I was on the cusp of some significant changes but couldn't identify exactly what it was I was doing, where I was headed, or what was happening to me. His smell permeated my clothes and his hungry kisses pulsed on my lips, days after having been intimate with him, I knew in my spirit that I had never tasted anything sweeter or partaken in anything more fulfilling, never had I been so free to let go.

The release felt good, healthy, like I had not only delivered what was growing inside of me, I had been delivered, reborn each time he penetrated me, each time he put his hands around my neck and consumed me. I was set free from the bondage of societal conditioning, and never once did I worry that it was wrong to feel or behave that way. It was the most natural thing in the world. I trusted him, and I trusted how I felt. I wanted to know more; I wanted him to teach me more.

I pulled into the parking lot of Lucas' office and stepped out feeling open, enlightened, intrigued, and rather deviant. Walking into his building, I pulled the sunglasses from my face. An old floral couch caught my eye, carpet cleaning machines and hoses were scattered about. A light was on in one of the offices, so I approached and leaned into the doorway. Lucas looked up and stood, inviting me in. I stepped forward. His strong, masculine hand enveloped mine, pulling it to his lips, he kissed it tenderly. His lips were warm and shooting electrical currents through my everything, especially down there. My pussy was purring like a happy kitten after some warm milk and a thorough petting. He stepped out of his office and locked the entryway door.

Moving effortlessly back through the doorway toward me, my confidence was replaced by anticipation. My back turned to him, Lucas' hands forced my hips forward into the ledge of his desk top. His hips pushing roughly into my rear end, he grabbed my hair, pushing my torso over. I heard his belt buckle jingling as he unbuckled, unbuttoned, and unzipped his black dress pants.

I felt his stiff warm member on the exposed skin of my lower back. He shoved me forward, pushing my chest and shoulders into his desk top forcefully,

"Who does this pussy belong to, little girl?" he growled, pressing his fingers into my crotch, rubbing it roughly through my jeans.

"It's yours," I moaned, my cheek smashed into the surface of his desk.

Grabbing the back of my hair, he pulled me up into a standing position.

"How are you to address me?" he inquired, his tone dripping with dominance.

"I am yours, Sir," I replied.

Lucas led me into the foyer, standing me in front of the couch. His hands roamed my body hungrily, his breathing labored. Lucas tugged at my jeans button and zipper. I helped him slip me out of my clothes.

"Are you sorry for forgetting?" he asked.

Turning me to face him, "Yes, Sir," I replied.

He kissed me passionately and my body turned to Jell-O. We swayed together, tangled flailing arms, legs, and tongues lashing at one another furiously. Lucas pushed me onto the couch, smiled a deviant smile, and yanked my legs apart.

He buried his face and tongue into my wetness. My hands found my hair and tugged at it as my head and eyes rolled backward. Moans escaped my body as wave after wave of pleasure wove their way through my body. Each roll of his tongue across my clit was absolutely sinful.

"Oh god... Uh-huh. Yeah-Yeah-Yeah," I whimpered.

He started to get rough, biting down hard on my clit. It became uncomfortable.

"Ow," I breathed. "N-No... No, No, No... Please, don't," I urged.

Lucas slid from between my thighs and plunged into me. Any and all pain was forgiven and forgotten immediately.

"Ugh," we both grunted as he pushed inside.

He placed my legs over his shoulders and bent me in half as he fucked me savagely. I felt like I was going to pass out from the pleasure. I could barely breath and I couldn't speak.

"I-I," I stuttered.

"Tell me," Lucas taunted as he plunged harder and harder into my recesses.

"Fuh-Fuck, Ugh-I, Mmm, I-f-feel, li-like-Uhmmm..."

"Say it, little girl; how does this cock make you feel?"

He demanded my answer, grabbing my chin and kissing me, drenching my face in his sweat and spit. I grabbed my hair, squeezing my eyes shut to focus.

Holding my breath for a moment, I attempted to continue, "I fee-feel, like... like... mmm, like- its cuh-coming out-out... Oh my god!" I cried.

He slowed his stroke to a steady rhythmic pounding. I could feel every inch of him sliding in and out of me.

"Tell me, how much you love this cock," he commanded, his voice deep and sinister.

Lucas sweetly stroked away the sweat-drenched hair that had matted itself to my face.

"My-Mm, my-Mouth. I feel like it's coming out of my mouth," I managed to finally spit it out.

Lucas growled and slammed into me with all of his might.

"FUCK," I screamed at the top of my lungs.

Tears streamed from my eyes. My head bobbed from side to side as he devastated my pussy.

"Oh my god, Oh my god," I mumbled over and over while he demolished me.

It was all I could muster.

"Yes, little girl, you called my name?" I smiled weakly at his cockiness.

10

Chapter 10

We were now many months into our regular rendezvous. I had finally been offered the opportunity to meet some of Lucas' friends. He said we were going to have a few casual drinks with a couple named Pam and Frank. We were on our way to their home when Lucas grabbed my hand from across the truck and brought my fingers to his mouth. I watched his lips and tongue trail my knuckles and down my fingers. Smiling, I scooted over and brushed his neck with my nose. I exhaled my hot breath into his jaw line, allowing a small moan to escape as I nibbled and licked.

"Mmm, baby, I will pull this truck over and fuck that little ass, don't start something you aren't willing to finish," he breathed in his deep gruff voice.

I smiled and giggled, sliding back over to my side of the vehicle to secure my seat belt over my chest. Lucas smiled back. I stared straight ahead for the rest of the silent ride to Lucas's friends' house. I was nervous and happy. He was finally introducing me to his friends. I felt that this was a significant moment, even though it was only very casual drinks—as he had put it. It was a start, and Lucas was letting me in some.

"Here we are." Lucas' voice sliced into my day dream and I jumped. "You okay?" he inquired, concerned.

"Uh-Yep… Mhm! I-I'm fine," I stuttered, blushing.

"You sure?" he insisted.

I laughed nervously, "Yes."

He stared at me for a moment longer. I straightened my hair and held tightly to my purse.

"Shall we?"

Lucas opened the truck door.

"Yea-Yes…" I smiled.

He made his way over to the passenger side and let me out, helping me down. He hugged my waist tight with one arm as we made our way up the driveway.

Lucas pressed the doorbell and it sounded throughout the rather large home. An entryway light flipped on, and then the porch light. A towering middle-aged football player looking man opened the door.

"Hey, hey! Come on in, you two! Lucas!" The man nodded his head in acknowledgement and shook his hand.

A woman appeared, tan, middle-aged, short blonde curly hair, about 5'4". She greeted me warmly with a tight hug and introduced herself as Pam. Her husband grabbed my hand and kissed it looking intently into my eyes,

"And this beauty must be the lovely Amber. My name is Frank."

I blushed and looked at Lucas. He smiled endearingly at me.

"You would be correct," Lucas responded, pulling me to his side.

I snuggled into his firm grip, placing my hand on his abdomen.

"A pleasure to meet you, Pam… Frank," I nodded graciously. "Thank you for inviting us over."

"The pleasure is all mine; I am sure, sweetheart." Frank winked at me as we trailed behind Pam and Lucas who were already seating themselves in the living room.

I had a growing feeling of uncertainty. These friends of Lucas' were extremely friendly, and excessively 'handsy'. What created even more confusion was that Lucas seemed to be fine with it.

I sat in a chair across the room from Lucas because Pam had taken a seat directly beside him on the sofa. There was that uncomfortable feeling that I couldn't quite put my finger on again. A hand touched my shoulder. I jumped so hard the wooden legs of the chair made a screeching sound as it scrubbed against the wood floor, everyone laughed.

"I apologize. I didn't mean to startle you. Would you like a drink, Amber?" Frank inquired.

I tucked my hair behind my ear and managed an embarrassed smile.

"Yes, please, thank you." I cleared my throat.

All eyes were on me from across the room as Frank disappeared behind the bar to make the cocktails.

"She is truly lovely, Lucas. Those freckles and that long red hair, mmm."

Pam bit her lower lip and looked at me lustfully. My stomach lurched, my heart began to race, my mind matching its rhythm–thoughts ping ponged off my skull–nothing really making enough sense to sink in. *What?* I thought to myself. *Is this what I think it is? Am I meeting a couple that he has been with before? What is happening, this was supposed to just be drinks?"* I contemplated.

Pam touched Lucas' leg, trailing her fingers toward his zipper. Lucas remained still, staring at me. Our eyes made contact. I knew he had to see the confusion, the gleam of jealousy, the curiosity... Frank delivered the cocktail and broke the flow of poison darts shooting from my gaze into Pam's and Lucas' souls.

"Drinks for everyone!" he sang into the silence.

I took the drink, smiling politely at Frank so as not to make everyone uncomfortable with my increasing irritation and confusion.

He handed Lucas and Pam their drinks and made his way back over to me.

"What kind of music do you listen to, Amber?"

Frank took a sip of his drink and sat it down on the glass table between us and began to rub my shoulders. I got cold chills all over my body. Lucas' facial expression didn't change at all as he sipped his beer. He was watching his friend touch me. My entire body tensed. I wasn't at all comfortable with this situation, as it was becoming more and more obvious that I had been lured into meeting a couple for sex. I struggled with this knowledge in great part because, the act of luring me into a situation wasn't necessary. Lucas knew I would do anything to please him, so why lie, and essentially trap me in a sexual situation?

"I-um, I listen to a little bit of everything," I managed to stumble out, unable to take my eyes off Lucas and Pam.

"That is terrific! You have eclectic tastes. I like that; a woman that doesn't limit herself."

Frank leaned down, breathing his words into my hair. I lowered my eyes to the left, feeling his hot breath radiating through my hair and onto the skin of my neck. My lips parted as I took in a sharp breath. He had reached around and pulled my hair to the side. I made eye contact again with Lucas. The look on his face had changed to dark and predatory. He was laser beam focused on my eyes, he wanted to see my response to Frank.

Pam began touching herself. Lucas slowly reached over and took Pam's hand from between her thighs and placed it on his very erect member. Frank tugged my head to the side gently and kissed my neck. I sucked down my drink and Frank took the glass from me, sitting it down on the table beside his. He ran his tongue up my neck. Pam had gotten down on her knees before Lucas and was pulling his cock out of his slacks. Our eyes burned into each other's as Pam's head bobbed up and down on his shaft. I noted Lucas' hips began to swivel slightly. He was enjoying her mouth.

Frank stood me up, roughly grabbing my breasts from behind. I watched Lucas place his hand on Pam's head, close his eyes, and lean his head back. I was becoming aroused, so I took my cue from him, closed my eyes, and leaned my head into Frank's broad chest. The alcohol was seeping into my bloodstream. I licked my lips and began to relax; I was adjusting to the unfolding situation. I writhed my body into his as his hands found their way down the front of my jeans. His fingers made heavenly circles on my clit. I moaned softly as I felt

Frank's erection in the small of my back.

Pam had pulled her breasts out and was touching herself with one hand while using the other to squeeze her breasts as she serviced Lucas' cock. He was now focused on me again; letting his brooding dark brown eyes drift from Frank's hand down my jeans, then to his mouth exploring my body, and back to my face. He took a sip of his beer and stopped Pam.

"Undress yourself and lie down on the rug."

Pam did as she was told.

"Spread your legs."

She complied.

"Wider," Lucas spoke softly.

She did as he requested again. I marveled at his ability to make pretty much any woman do whatever he said. It turned me on.

Lucas looked at me, "Come to me."

He held his hand out. I removed Frank's hand from my pants and walked toward my god, no questions asked.

I took Lucas' hand and he pulled me roughly toward him. He turned me around to face Pam.

"Look at her."

I did as I was told. Pam began to rub her breasts.

"Don't touch yourself. Lie flat and still. Keep your legs spread."

Pam let out a soft whimper of protest but complied.

"I want you to fuck her."

I bit my lower lip and closed my eyes, leaning my head into his mouth. His words were like drinking an entire bottle of vodka.

I nodded that I understood, "Yes Sir."

Frank had made his way across the room and knelt on the Mohair Rug, stroking his cock. I slid to my knees and crawled around to Pam's spread eagle legs. Sitting back on my knees, I let my eyes drift over her body. She was beautiful, shapely, a stunning middle-aged woman. She had taken very good care of herself through the years. I had been with a high school girlfriend intimately before. Lucas did not know this just yet. I had never mentioned it because it had never become relevant. But the truth was, I had so many crushes on girls from a very young age; so being with a woman was, as Frank put it, "my pleasure". I ran my hands down her body, squeezing her supple thighs. I kissed her passionately and moved to her neck, where I bit down on her jaw line as I pulled her hair. She was mine in that moment. I was his and she was mine.

11

Chapter 11

It had been so long since I had been with a woman, and I didn't realize that I was starving until I tasted her. I became this insatiable beast with food aggression, and I had prime rib before me. As I fucked her, I caught glimpses of moments, and at one point, Pam's legs were straight up in the air, toes pointed and curled, thighs and calves rock hard; her moans garbled and incoherent. Frank shoved himself inside of me after I batted his hands away from my prize. His time inside of me was a series of hyper focused thrusting and a version of blind frantic groping of my ass cheeks, lifting and spreading them so I was wide open for his probing.

Lucas watched me devour her with his cock in Pam's mouth. She suckled at it between moans. He kept pulling her head toward his member in countless attempts to keep her focused on his pleasure, but she was not having it. Finally, she just gripped his softening cock with her hand and tugged at it weakly while alternating between watching me lick her pussy and throwing her head back, her eyes rolling in their sockets. Lucas pulled himself free and headed my way. I heard mumbling behind me and then Frank was no longer inside of me. I felt my god's body heat from inches away. He was getting situated, I could sense it. I felt my pussy contract and release, contract and release. It was throbbing in anticipation of him.

Lucas ran his hand down my back. I leaned my head down and

rested my left cheek on Pam's inner thigh. I knew he would take my breath when he put himself inside of me. He had never failed to thus far. Pam ran her hands through the mess of my red curls signaling her desperation for me to please not stop. Her hips ground into my face. But I didn't care what she wanted in that moment. This moment was MINE alone. He was preparing to plug himself into me and fill me.

I pushed away from Pam's thighs and sat upright on my knees. Extending my arms over my head, I pulled Lucas to me. I clasped my hands around the back of his neck as he explored my neck and jawline with his mouth. I was dripping for him. As if he sensed my condition, he placed himself inside of me while Frank stood off to the side, stroking his reddish-purple cock head. Pam fingered her glistening pussy, whimpering, desperate to cum. My body tensed and writhed. The pleasure tapped into my wild, my dark, my aching; it was so fulfilling, so needed, and so appreciated.

The alcohol had kicked in all of the way. My face was numb, I felt no pain, and had no inhibitions.

"Yes, yes, fuck me, please," I cried out.

My eyes were now closed, my head leaning back on Lucas' strong right shoulder, neck exposed for his pleasure—just as it should be. I was his to do with as he pleased. He was deep inside of me, barely moving in and out but giving me every inch and then some. My greedy pussy tightening and craving more, deeper, harder, faster, the desire was killing me.

"P-Please, more, harder, Sir." I breathed into Lucas's neck.

"Yeah?" He taunted me.

"Yes. Yea-Yes Sir," I stuttered, leaning forward to place my hands on the floor.

He allowed me to fall forward and pushed my shoulders hard into the rug. Frank groaned and motioned for Pam to come tend to his member with her mouth. My ass was in the air, thighs wide apart, back arched, shoulders and face smashed into the carpet, arms stretched out in front of me. Frank and Pam made their way over to the sofa where Lucas and she had sat earlier. Pam climbed atop Frank and began riding him.

"God, you are so fucking wet, baby," he groaned to his wife while looking at me looking at him from the view between the long fibers of their rug.

His lips curled back as Lucas gathered my hair, gently, into a low ponytail. He knew I was about to get it, and I was about to get it good. Frank was a bit of a savage in a Hyena-ish kind of way. I watched Frank's cock glide in and out of Pam in between my vision going blurry from my eyes rolling into the back of my head, and drifting wherever they may. I didn't fucking care that I probably looked possessed. I was possessed. I was possessed and overtaken, I was drowning in my god and I didn't give two fucks that he was absorbing my soul so long as he took me to that place where all was quiet, my reality was no more; that place where my soul dragged her terrified ass out of my mouth and flung herself as far away from me as possible.

Lucas plunged into me again and again. All I could do was lie there, holding my breath, and be demolished. My body was too weak to move, even a centimeter. I lay there with my face burning from sliding back and forth on their carpet, watching Frank sneer at me and fuck his wife harder every time my eyes rolled into my head. He grunted and slammed into Pam. She hurriedly hopped off him and caught what she could of her husband's spurting fluids in her mouth and on her breasts. She made smacking and gurgling sounds as Frank finished his orgasm and moaned louder than any man I had ever heard.

Lucas slapped my ass and growled softly for me to turn over onto my back. My body slid the rest of the way to the floor and he helped me turn over. He threw my legs over his shoulders and possessively yanked my bottom into his pelvis, dragging me across the carpet. I let my arms lie loose above my head. He pushed into me forcefully, thrusting his hips forward, fast and hard. He wanted to cum. Rapid fire pounding into my cervix, my entire body tensed and writhed in pleasure. I pushed down and into him with each thrust inward, lifting my body from the floor, and squeezing him with my thighs. My back and shoulders were clear of the floor by a foot or so for the duration of this severe pounding.

Pam's muffled, " Fuck yes, fuck that pretty pussy. God, I wish I were you right now," in my ear roused me back down to Earth.

She swept the sweat-soaked strands of hair from my face and kissed me deeply. Her tongue felt swollen and slimy. It was still covered in Frank's semen. Frank moaned at the sight of a string of his cum connecting his wife and myself as she broke away from the kiss. He rubbed his slowly swelling and rising member. I felt a bit sick to my stomach, I wasn't crazy about his taste; it tasted of chlorine.

I did my best to hold my queasiness in and avoided kissing Pam and making contact with Frank for the rest of our time in their home. Lucas didn't finish with me. He ended up giving Pam his orgasm, which I felt quite irritated by, as we said our goodbyes to the couple. I felt unsatisfied, getting into the truck to head home. I was very quiet until Lucas broke the silence.

"So, you are quite the pussy hog; what's up with that?"

I looked down, my pout session pausing for a beaming smile. I glanced over at him, serving my best innocent face, and shrugged playfully.

12

Chapter 12

For the first time, I saw surprise pass over his face. I relished in that small victory. I had finally managed to catch Lucas off guard and there was no way I was going to allow this to go unnoticed. He made me highly uncomfortable on a regular basis, and it was finally my moment in the moonlight; it sure as shit felt incredible.

Lucas' diesel rumbled into my quiet suburban neighborhood, coming to a stop in front of my house. It was well after midnight. No porch light on; my mother must have fallen asleep watching television again. He shut off the truck. A dog started barking, breaking the silence that fell over us. I stared out the window, feeling sadness settle in that it was time to part ways until next time; whenever next time would be.

Lucas touched my hand and then grasped it, pulling it and me toward him. My attention turned to his face, his smoldering dark brown eyes burning into mine. I slid closer to him so that our bodies were touching. He, still holding onto my hand, brought it to his mauve lips, and brushed his greying 5 o' clock shadow over my knuckles.

My insides quivered and sighed at the same time. I couldn't break his gaze, even if I wanted to. I felt myself become instantly wet, dripping even down there. I wanted him so badly that my pussy was contracting with such severity it hurt. He let go of my hand and grabbed my chin, pulling my face to his ever so gently. I closed my eyes, enjoying the tender tantric moment our lips met. He devoured a bit more of my soul.

I pressed my lips against his, hard. My body followed up by straddling him and grinding my hips into his semi-erect cock. I wanted him again, I wanted him in vicious and ferocious ways. I longed for his presence inside of me so deeply it physically hurt. He was the only one that could make it hurt and take away the pain all the same. He had become my drug. Without him, I was strung out and suffering from withdrawal.

He grabbed two handfuls of my ass and spread me open, just the way he loved, in the way that brought forth that primal groan and growl I so adored; wide open and dripping inside of my jeans, ready to take him into me. I felt his hard cock pressing into my crotch, driving me to the brink of insanity if he didn't allow me to have him. I needed it.

"It hurts," I whispered into his ear with shuddering breaths.

Lucas pushed into me harder.

"What hurts, little girl?" he inquired.

"I want you so fucking bad. I want you so bad it hurts down there."

Taking his hand, I guided it to my pussy. He felt my desire seeping through my clothes and growled, grabbing a handful of my hair. My back pressed into the steering wheel, he held me there, my hips grinding into him. Lucas pushed me into him harder as he unbuckled my jeans and slid his right hand down the front of them, into my wetness. He snaked three fingers inside of me. I cried out in pain. He let my hair go and covered my mouth.

I breathed heavily into his left hand, never taking my eyes off his as his fingers maneuvered expertly inside of my walls until I came, whimpering into the palm of his hand.

"Whose pussy is this?" Lucas hissed as he pulled his hand from my jeans and placed those same three fingers into my mouth. "Tell me whose pussy this is, NOW!" he hissed again.

I stuttered, my mouth full of his thick fingers. "Yours, yours. It's yours."

He removed his fingers from my mouth and grabbed my neck, pulling me to him, and kissing me deeply.

"You're goddamn right it's mine; that's my good girl."

He pulled his face from mine and looked into my eyes, repeating softly and earnestly, "Good girl, that's my good girl."

Ease washed over me, a sense of well-being, and accomplishment. I had done the right thing and was rewarded. I was a good girl; I was HIS good girl. My heart was full. We had a moment.

There was no doubt about it; we had a fucking moment; right there, just then. The Oxytocin—we were drenched in it from the inside out. It ran through his fingertips, into my skin, and coated my entire being. I pressed my forehead against his as Lucas tenderly pulled my hair into a low ponytail. We closed our eyes. I took his right hand from my lower back and brought it to my mouth, kissing his fingers adoringly.

I mumbled into his forehead, "I don't..."

I felt overcome, overwhelmed all of a sudden. Tears came to my eyes and I couldn't breathe. There was a large lump obstructing my airways.

He took my face from his to look at me full-on.

"You're shaking, what's wrong?" he inquired.

His eyes searched mine. I looked down feeling terrible that I had worried him, feeling terrible and embarrassed that I was getting emotional.

"No, no, no, no. Don't cry, shhh."

He held me to his chest and the flood gates opened. I sat there straddling him, sopping wet in the crotch, jeans unbuttoned and unzipped, halfway down, my ass out, snot flowing, full on sobbing. He held me tightly until I calmed down enough to finish my sentence. I leaned back, taking the tissue he had pulled out of his door's side compartment. Wiping my nose with one, and my eyes with the other, I let out a shuddering breath, attempting to calm myself enough to speak.

"That's it, breathe. Deep breaths," Lucas coached me.

In through your nose, out through your mouth until all of the air is out of your lungs. Slowly, Amber, slowly, I coached myself.

"I...," I began, as I wiped at my stuffed up nose. "I don't understand," I continued.

Lucas rubbed my thigh.

"What don't you understand, Amber?"

I looked at him with my swollen, makeup-smeared eyes. I tugged at my pants, pulling them up as much as I could before untangling myself from him and plopping down onto the grey leather bench seat at his side.

I buttoned and zipped my pants and folded my hands in my lap, staring down at them as I turned the wadded napkins over and over, squeezing them into tight balls. Lucas touched my chin. I looked at him. He looked back at me expectantly.

"I just-I don't understand how you make me feel things like-just... everything all at once," I gushed.

He looked straight forward, his jaw taut. His expression changed to nothingness.

After what seemed an eternity, he spoke in a tone of grave seriousness, "You cannot fall in love with me, Amber."

I died on the inside and I know he saw the lights go out in my eyes, as immediately, the regret set in that I had not only lost my shit in his lap, I then proceeded to pour out the contents of my soul to him. I was dying, I was sure of it. In that moment, I was melting into a puddle of primordial ooze and seeking asylum in Hell.

I was mad at myself. I was embarrassed. I knew better. I got caught up. That was my bad.

Lucas was witnessing me melt down on the inside, so I attempted to recover.

"Um, yeah. I-I totally understand. I mean, you're married. I-I get it. It's totally fine. It's fine. It's fine..."

I nodded furiously, faking a smile and nervously grabbing at my things to get the fuck out of there before I said it's totally fine, again.

Amber, get it the fuck together like, NOW, I mentally berated myself.

"You know, I'm just gonna-" I pointed my thumb toward my front porch, opened the door, and stumbled out of the truck. "I'm sorry. I'm fine," I squeaked. "I'm just gonna um, thank-thanks for tonight, bye."

I shut the truck door a little bit too hard and waved an apology, walking awkwardly away, as fast as I could.

13

Chapter 13

Eight days of silence; not a peep from Lucas.

Why would he want anything to do with me after the way I had acted? I might be freaked out too if someone had snotted and ugly cried on me, then decided it was acceptable to confess feelings after only a handful of months' worth of trysts and rendezvous. That is all it was, Amber; nothing more, nothing less than two adults fucking. Deal with it and get your act together.

I beat myself up every second of every one of those eight days. I was certain I had lost him for good.

You can't lose something that was never yours to have in the first place, idiot. Hello, can we say, married? I screamed at myself.

I rolled my eyes and carried my misery parade and beef flavored Ramen noodle soup to my room. Flopping down on my bed, I noticed the notification light was blinking on my cell. I took a bite of my noodles and proceeded to check my phone.

It was a missed call, from him. No voicemail. I stopped chewing and swallowed the rather large bite of food I had crammed into my mouth with an audible gulp. I felt my entire body flush. The hair raised on the top of my head with such ferocity that it felt as if someone were lightly running their fingers through it. There was no deciding about it, I was calling him back.

"Okay, okay, okay," I whispered aloud as I clicked on his name to return the call.

It's ringing, I said in my head.

I placed my hand on my forehead and squeezed my eyes shut. Rubbing the protruding vein in the center of my forehead, the ringing stopped, and I heard his voice.

"Sure-Clean, this is Lucas," he answered.

"Hey, Hi-It's Amber. I saw that I um, had a missed call from you?" I inquired nervously. "You didn't leave a voicemail, so… I-I thought I-you um–"

Lucas cut me off. "I made a profile for us. It's on a swingers lifestyle site. We've had quite a few hits, lots of messages and winks, people asking all about you."

His voice was animated in a way I had only heard before when he spoke of his "friends" that we were going to have "casual drinks" with.

"There is a couple that seems really down to Earth and fun. Would you be interested in having some dinner and drinks tonight with them?" Lucas inquired.

"Uh, I-yeah. Yes, I can do dinner and drinks," I replied, unsure of everything about the situation except that I really wanted to see him again.

He told me that the couple's names were Gemma and Andrew. He also seemed exceptionally enthusiastic about this pair. He insisted I would adore Gemma. He told me they loved the pictures of me. When I inquired about where he got pictures of me, he explained that he had taken some from my social media profile and uploaded them onto our profile on the website.

I wasn't aware that he had sought me out on social media. I smiled broadly as we finalized plans and hung up.

He has been stalking me online. How about them apples? I mentally patted myself on the back.

My entire mood had shifted from doom and gloom to excitement. Short of him canceling plans, there was nothing that could bring me down. We were back, well, sort of. Without expectations, and feelings, and hopes of anything serious ever happening between us.

Truthfully, I felt a bit indifferent about it all but managed to brush it off and get ready for my evening with Lucas, my god, the bane of my existence—until he cast his gaze in my direction.

* * *

2 hours later...

I took a deep breath as I slid my arm through Lucas' and walked into the dimly lit Italian restaurant. The hostess asked if there were only two dining.

"We are with a party, there will be four. Perhaps, they are already seated. Do you mind if we look?" Lucas inquired with a dashing smile.

The hostess flushed and subtly swooned as she stuttered, "B-by all means, please do."

Lucas nodded a polite thank you and we went in search of Gemma and Andrew, but not before I gave the hostess a telepathic piece of my mind, and the watchful side eye, as I purposely trailed behind. We turned the corner, and Lucas recognized them immediately.

Gemma, a stunning, busty, blond-haired, blue-eyed beauty stood when her husband, Andrew, a mousy, dishwater brown haired, accountant type, gently patted her arm upon seeing Lucas. I appeared beside him just in time to see Gemma rise from her seat and smile a brilliant, gleaming, smile that lit up her entire face. Our eyes locked, I was mesmerized and awe-struck by how stunning she was. I gravitated toward her and she pulled me into a tight hug, pressing her body into mine seductively. She smelled incredible, *Clinique's 'Happy'*. I stepped back from the hug to acknowledge her husband, and she held my hand affectionately, never taking her eyes off me.

"Andrew, nice to meet you, I'm Amber."

I shook his hand and he leaned in to give me a one-armed hug, followed by an uncomfortable peck on the cheek. I laughed a nervous laugh and turned my attention back to Gemma. I kissed her cheek and let her know I was going to take a seat. The waiter came around and got our drink orders. Lucas was still standing, awaiting my return to his side. I met up with him on the other side of the table. He kissed my forehead endearingly and pulled out my chair. Inside, I was squealing with delight.

"Such a gentleman," I whispered seductively in his ear.

He leaned into whisper in mine, "Your ass is mine later."

My pussy clenched tight and became instantly wet. My cheeks flushed, and I smiled as I tucked my hair behind my ear, in an effort to recompose my now flustered self.

"We love you guys' pictures online. But the pictures do not do Amber justice. She truly is so much more beautiful in person," Gemma gushed to Lucas.

Andrew nodded his agreement as he took a sip of his red wine.

The waiter returned with our drinks. Lucas pulled me closer and smiled at me. I returned his smile, adoring him.

"She is really into you," he muttered into my ear, making eye contact with Gemma as he spoke to me.

His lips were cold from the beer he had been nursing on since we sat down. She took a sip of her wine, seductively peering over the goblet at the both of us. Those were definitely 'Fuck Me Now' eyes.

"What wine are you drinking, Gemma?" I inquired so as to break some of the sexual tension that Andrew was clearly not included in thus far.

Her face lit up as she smiled broadly.

"It is called, *Menag a Trois*. It is a delicious blend of three sweeter red wines. Would you like to try some?"

She offered me her glass.

"Oh, no thank you. Red wines usually give me a bad headache," I replied.

Her face fell. "Oh, it must be the tannin in the wines that you have tried. *Menag a Trois* is a very good wine. Won't you try just a sip for me?"

Her big blue eyes begged my lips to press against her glass. I looked at

Lucas, he sipped his beer, and struck up a conversation with Andrew.

"Okay, just a sip wouldn't hurt, I suppose."

I caved and took her glass. She clapped her hands happily and swore I would be converted to a red wine drinker after having tried it.

"It is quite delicious."

I nodded my approval. Surprisingly, it was something I wouldn't mind having more of in the future.

"You have shown me something new, Gemma, thank you."

She beamed at me, "I just knew you'd love it."

The waiter circled around again, nodding so as to say, 'Another?'

I held my glass up and off he went. He returned moments later with another Amaretto Sour. "Thank you," I mouthed.

He bowed his head saying, "You're welcome Miss."

Gemma piped up, saying the hotel they were staying in had incredible sheets and a heated pool. She suggested we all head that way for a night cap. Lucas looked at me. I looked at Lucas. Andrew looked briefly at his wife, and then to my breasts, and then nervously to my face, and then to Lucas who was now giving Gemma the 'sex eyes'. She smiled deviantly into her last sip of *Menag a Trois*.

"Do you want to go with them?" I whispered to Lucas.

"Do you?" he whispered back, never taking his eyes off Gemma's.

I looked at Andrew. He looked at me and smiled sheepishly. I looked at Gemma, entranced by Lucas' piercing gaze.

"I have to go to the bathroom, excuse me," I announced abruptly.

I stood up, Lucas and Andrew stood up.

Gemma chimed in, "Oh! I should powder my nose as well. Excuse us boys, we have to go gossip about you now."

She tossed her thick blonde mane over her shoulder and shot a wink at me as she took my arm, and we headed toward the restrooms.

I pee'd and came out of the stall to wash my hands. Gemma was applying more lipstick.

"Lucas is dreamy, Amber! You are a lucky girl. I bet he is amaaaaaazzzzingggg in bed, am I right?"

Her face was animated, she stopped applying the lipstick to hear my response.

"I- yes, he is the best lover I have ever had."

Gemma sighed, "I knew it. He just gives off that vibe. Some guys, you can just tell, ya know?"

I nodded in agreement as I pulled about ten too many paper towels out of the dispenser to dry my hands.

"These-stupid dispensers," I muttered and threw a massive wad of the damp towels away.

I turned to leave, and Gemma stood between me and the door, looking at me with her best 'take me now' eyes.

I froze in my tracks, unsure of what was okay to do and what wasn't in this situation. After a moment of processing, I decided to politely leave the bathroom and go back to the table. I smiled and stepped forward, touching her hip to gently urge her to step aside and let me pass. I opened my mouth and managed to get out, "Excuse Mm-" when her tongue was shoved into my face and began probing the inside of my mouth. It was luscious and warm. It slid over mine like silk over freshly shaven legs. The gloves were off now, she touched me, and I was no longer responsible for how I responded.

I grabbed a handful of her abundant ass and pulled her into me, backing her into the counter. She moaned softly and began breathing heavily, as her hands pawed at the bottom of my shirt. Taking her hand away from my abdomen, I held it above her head while my other hand wrapped itself in the thickness of the hair at the nape of her neck, tugging her head slightly back and to the side.

I bit into the softness of Gemma's neck, the delicious part in between that connects the shoulder to the neck. She writhed, and squirmed, and moaned, and panted. I kissed and licked my way up to her jawline where I bit her again, scraping my teeth just enough to cause a small amount of stinging pain with her pleasure. She moaned again, this time a bit louder. I heard the bathroom door swing open and I released her.

70

Gemma slumped onto the countertop, loosely holding herself upright. I gave her a wink as I made my exit. The woman that had entered the restrooms gave us a questioning look and brushed past me to enter a stall. I approached the table; Lucas and Andrew both stood. Lucas pulled my chair out for me, scooting me in.

"You're flushed," he said softly in my ear and laughed.

I had a perma-grin on my face until we all left the restaurant to head to Gemma and Andrew's hotel room.

Once in their room and situated, the men went downstairs to have a few more beers while us girls got a bit more comfortable. Gemma and I hopped into the bed and began to snuggle and giggle. The alcohol was firmly in my bloodstream and hitting hard.

Gemma turned to face me, "Let's take a shower together! I've always wanted to shower with a girl."

I jumped out of bed and immediately headed for the bathroom.

"I'll get the water going for us!" I called out.

"Thank you, sweetheart!" she called back.

The shower was running, and the water was perfect.

"Water's up to temp!" I called out.

Gemma strolled into the bathroom, absolutely nude.

My breath caught in my throat. Her everything was magnificent. She was curvy, her breasts, thighs, and ass all ample and edible. I wanted to fuck her right then and there. She pulled me into the shower with her. I watched her blonde hair turn a couple shades darker as the water cascaded down her tanned body. She turned around to face me and laughed as she inquired if all I was going to do was stare at her.

I said, "I can't help myself, you are stunning. And you have water trickling down your body, you're all soapy... and..."

I stopped talking to caress her skin and kiss her.

I pulled away.

"And what?" Gemma inquired softly.

I turned her around to face away from me, grabbing the soap from her hands.

I washed her gorgeous breasts as I whispered into her neck, "I need to lick your pussy right now. So, let's get you washed, rinsed, and in the bed."

I nipped at her neck.

"Ugh! god, the goosebumps you give me when you do that!!!! No woman has ever given me the chills like you do."

I smiled as I turned off the shower.

14

Chapter 14

"A towel for you!" Gemma chirped happily.

I smiled at her, taking the towel.

"And a towel for me."

She dried her hair and wrapped her body in it. As she made her way out of the bathroom, Gemma called out, asking if I would like another drink.

"Sure, I'll take another, thanks."

"You got it, sweetie!" she sang back.

I loved her energy, she seemed so happy and upbeat, yet there was a more mysterious, sexy, sensual side that shone through from time to time. It made me curious to find out what this mysterious side consisted of. I was going to find out.

Gemma handed me my drink and we toasted to new friendships and great sex. We looked one another in the eyes as we drank our beverages down. I leaned forward to sit my drink down, and she swallowed hard. I placed it on the table behind her, and stood tall and squarely in front of her, staring intently into her beautiful blue eyes. I reached out and un-tucked her towel, allowing it to drop to the floor.

"I-I'm a pillow princess. I-I don't know how to go down on another girl. I don't even know if I'd like it," she touted nervously, backing away, and attempting to scoot around me.

I followed her, slowly-deliberately.

73

She bumped into the bed, stumbling.

"I-I've never had a good experience with a woman. S-so, I'm kind of nervous," she stuttered.

The once confident, seductive blonde scooted backward onto the bed. I crept onto the king-sized bed, crawling and creeping silently like a leopard readying itself to pounce. Gemma held herself up on her elbows, watching me. I never took my eyes off of hers.

I sat back on my knees, admiring her beauty from head to toe. Trailing my hands up her calves and thighs, I slid my body atop hers, snake-like, barely brushing her pussy with my lips and hair. I exhaled my hot alcohol-laden breath onto her slightly protruding clit. Gemma took in a sharp breath and exhaled a moan as I bit her inner left thigh.

I smiled into her thigh, licking my way to her wetness. I held her gaze as I swung my hair over my right shoulder and slid my tongue softly, tantalizingly, expertly, over her pussy lips. Her body rolled in response. She clenched the pillow with one hand and the sheet with the other. Stroke after stroke, flick after flick of my tongue, her hips rocked, and her thighs clamped over my ears. Her hands clawed at my hair as she whimpered my name, begging me to not stop.

A beer bottle clanked down on the table in the background. It was him, my god… He was standing behind me.

"I want that ass in the air now," Lucas demanded.

Deliberately disobedient, I grabbed Gemma's hips and pulled her pussy into my mouth hungrily-greedily. I felt her walls tighten around my fingers.

"Uh, Mm! Yes, yes, yes."

A gush of warm liquid flushed out of her contracting pussy and her rigid arched body fell into the bed in a well-fucked heap. I then untangled myself from her hips and pulled her up to me for a deep kiss as I looked directly into Lucas' eyes, defiantly.

"You smell so good," she purred into my neck, snuggling me.

"You taste so fucking good," I growled seductively into her ear, giving it a playful bite, then turning my attention to Andrew.

In a bold move, Andrew began rubbing the head of his hardening cock. Lucas took the final sip of his beer and appeared disinterested in the situation. Both men had stripped themselves of their clothing at some point in mine and Gemma's time together. Both were standing there naked, one stroking his hard cock and the other seemed displeased. I knew he was displeased with me, he wouldn't even look at me.

I patted Gemma's rear end playfully, signaling for her to get off of me. She took the cue and slid off, flopping down happily onto her back with a sigh. She threw a relaxed arm over her head. Andrew made his way over to his wife and Gemma took him into her mouth. I eased over to Lucas and wrapped my arms around his waist. He touched my arm, signaling for me to let him go, and he turned his back to me to open another beer. My heart dropped into my stomach, it was heavy as a bowling ball. Fear, uncertainty, and shame set in.

"Follow me to the bathroom."

Lucas' voice was soft but stern. I searched his face for clues as to what was going to happen. He looked at Gemma finishing Andrew up and kissed the top of my head and then picked up his clothes. I watched for any sign that he was irritated. Did he snatch his clothes? Did he stand up rigidly? I couldn't read his energy. I just knew that something was off, and it wasn't a good thing. I moved my two bricks for feet into that bathroom, pulling on my clothes as I walked.

As I slid my pants on, Andrew grunted out his orgasm. I stopped to watch. Hearing a sharp click from the bathroom, I winced and looked. Lucas had snapped his fingers and was looking at me with a rather annoyed look on his face. I didn't even bother zipping or buttoning my pants. I walked toward him. As I approached, he grabbed my hand and yanked me into the bathroom.

15

Chapter 15

He shut the door gently so as not to alarm anyone and turned to me.

"Care to explain what the fuck that was in there?"

Lucas glared down at me.

"What are you talking about?" I snapped back.

"I gave you a command and you failed to do as you were told, Amber." Lucas fumed.

Feeling attacked, anger bubbled up and spilled forth out of my mouth.

"I failed? Who are you to tell me that I have failed at anything; you don't fucking own me," I hissed.

The alcohol had emboldened me, and his hostile approach touched a nerve made sensitive in my childhood. Lucas' face tightened, his eyebrows shot up and then furrowed down.

I immediately regretted my decision to mouth off, but there was no backing out, and there was no fucking way I was going to allow him to make me feel like a failure. So, I glared back at him, hands on my hips. In one swift movement, Lucas grabbed my throat and pushed me hard against the wall. My head slamming against it, pain coursed through my skull. He placed his face so close to mine I felt the spit land on my lips as he hissed into the side of my face.

"You are MINE. You will do as I say, when I say, how I say; do I make myself absofuckinglutely clear?"

It felt as though my body had become one with the wall in that moment. Every muscle was tensed. Lucas' behavior was shocking. I was scared, and I was admittedly slightly turned on.

His brutality made my pussy throb and ache. Lucas moved his mouth to linger just in front of mine. We stood, him holding me there, his grip relaxing some, the two of us breathing in each other's breaths.

"Do you understand me, young lady?" Lucas' voice breathy and tender, he whispered his words into my lips.

I replied softly, "Yes, Sir."

He touched his forehead to mine and closed his eyes, exhaling, but still holding me by the throat against the wall. I looked at him, watching him in this moment. And for reasons I couldn't articulate, not only was I now Zen calm, I felt closer to him than I ever had.

I sucked his spit from my lips, taking it into me. It was all okay now. It was gone, swallowed down.

I took care of it, it's fine. It's inside of me now and you don't have to carry it anymore. I can take it, Sir, I said to him in my mind, as I joined him in closing my eyes too.

Lucas brushed his lips across mine. Releasing his grip on my throat, his hands roamed my body. Suddenly, I was tugged free of my jeans and bent over the cold, white, porcelain sink, one hand on the mirror sliding down, the other hand flailing desperately behind me to pull him deeper into me.

"Fuck me, please, Sir," I whispered, running my fingers through his hair, and the other hand on his gorgeous right ass cheek, nails digging into his skin as he put himself inside of me.

He grabbed a handful of my hair, jerking my head sideways. Lucas pulled out and refused to put himself back inside of me. I fucking loved to hate when he wouldn't give me what I needed. He knew this and held himself just outside my pussy. I moved my ass toward his erect cock, attempting to force it in. He would not allow it. I wanted to beg him to fuck me into oblivion. I peered over my shoulder at him, my face expressing my desperation and pleading. He held me there for what seemed a couple of minutes, just looking at me. Slowly, he pushed into me, giving me only small doses of his cock at a time, applying more and more pressure as he gauged my response, until he was firmly planted in my cervix.

"You're feeling bratty tonight, aren't you, little girl? I have just the thing to fix that," Lucas said through gritted teeth.

He tightened his grip on my hair; I winced. Lucas pulled out of me, pausing to admire my ass-and then laid into me, pounding me so hard I had trouble keeping my balance.

"If you fall, I will spank your ass so hard you won't be able to sit comfortably for a week, straighten up," he barked.

I grabbed for whatever I could get my hands on. I grabbed for the towel rack, it fell off, clanging on the floor with a loud, echoing, metallic sound. I grabbed at the corners of the sink. My hands were slick with sweat and began sliding forward until my face ended up in the sink. Lucas held my face down, my left cheek smashed against the basin. I didn't care that my moans were at screaming level and some peaking at octaves I had never reached in all my life, until that point. I just didn't want him to stop.

"Your pussy feels so good wrapped around my cock, little girl. You're gonna make me fucking cum, you know that?" he growled.

"Mm," I moaned into the sink.

I couldn't formulate any words. I was reaching that blessed place where everything was fuzzy, and warm, and pulsing. My orgasm was at its peak, I was holding on for as long as I could, because I wanted to explode with him. I felt my insides bunch up and begin contracting as he leaned his head back and groaned this desperate, heart-wrenching sound; it was a wail, a weeping. He began orgasming as he felt my walls spasming around his cock.

Lucas pushed into me desperately until he collapsed forward across my back, his hips thrusting into me, pushing his cum deep inside, just the way I adored. I moaned and panted, pressing my pussy into his hips, taking every inch of him and then some. I needed it all.

He lay draped over me, breathing heavily, moaning quietly, his cock twitching inside of me until it had softened enough to fall out. I felt the both of us draining out of me, and it was delightful, and sinful, and lusty. It was absofuckinglutely filthy, and I loved every second.

16

Chapter 16

He released my face from the sink and stood upright, unsteadily. I remained bent over for a moment longer, my chest heaving, smiling into the porcelain. Raising myself up, I flipped my hair over to one side as I put my panties back on. We dressed silently and quickly composed ourselves with one last glance at one another before Lucas opened the bathroom door.

We walked out into the lamp lit hotel room to find two sets of eyes staring at us knowingly. Andrew was good and plastered, sporting a half deviant grin and a 'just been fucked' cockatoo hair do. Gemma was sitting, legs crossed, robe slightly agape, casually sipping a cocktail with a devious look on her face. My cheeks flushed even more than they already were. A shy half smile formed at the left corner of my mouth as Gemma and I made eye contact.

She smiled back and rose from her chair, swinging her hair over her shoulder. She approached me and planted a luscious wet kiss on my lips. I breathed in deep, inhaling her breath and pulled her into me. I wrapped my hands in her hair and gave a gentle tug. Gemma moaned a soft moan and broke away from the kiss. My left hand traveled down to the wetness between her thighs. I bit my lip and slid my fingers inside of her. Her legs began to tremble, so I moved her to the wall for stabilization.

I pulled her head to the side, exposing her neck. Devouring every inch of her neck and chin, I worked my way down to her beautiful breasts and back to up to her plump lips. Gemma grabbed two handfuls of her hair, her body writhing and pumping in rhythm to my fingers working in and out of her folds. I curved my fingers inside of her, stroking her G-spot. She began to slide down the wall. I caught her and moved her to the bed, bending her over. Plunging my fingers deep inside her slick contracting pussy, Gemma moaned loudly.

I slapped her ass so hard my hand stung. She grabbed the covers and cried muffled words into the bunched fabric. Working my fingers into her as deep and hard as I could, I rubbed her red swelling ass cheek. I bent over and kissed the fingerprints that had become quite visible on her flesh. So plump and warm, I couldn't resist, I bit her left ass cheek hard enough to make her cry out, as I pushed into her quaking pussy with all of my strength.

Gemma's head flew back. Her blonde hair whipping over her shoulder blades, she spread her arms out before her in surrender to the pleasure and pain. She let out an audible primal moan. She was free–released, and she was so stunning in her surrender. I grabbed her right hip and turned my hand over, palm down, curving my fingers to firmly hit another G spot. Slowing the pace, more deliberate strokes. I placed my hips behind her ass cheeks. I slammed my hips into her ass as I pushed my arched fingers deep inside of her. Pausing between each stroke, for a heightened sense of anticipation and pleasure.

She bucked her pussy into my fingers, greedily, wanting more; wanting me deeper inside of her. I gave her every centimeter of me, every ounce of my effort and desire. Her hair stuck to her face. I rolled her over and climbed atop her, brushing her beautiful blue eyes clear of her blonde strands. Kissing her deeply, I rubbed my body all over hers, devouring her.

Feeling my god's hands on my hips, I stopped and looked over my shoulder to meet his honey brown eyes. They always changed when we were touching. Dinner, drinks, casual situations, his eyes were this dark brown, almost black, in color. When the clothes were off, his eyes were pools of honey and amber.

He pressed my shoulders into Gemma's hips.

"Please her."

His voice seeped into my psyche. I snaked my body down Gemma's, backing my ass into Lucas' waiting hips. He removed my pants once again, leaving my panties in place. He took the last swig of his beer and stretched to set the bottle down on the table adjacent to him, making certain that his hard cock remained in contact with my left ass cheek. Andrew looked to Lucas for direction and shuffled closer to my face. He touched my hair after searching Lucas' face for approval. Forcefully pushing her thighs open, I dove into Gemma's beautiful pussy. I cut my eyes at Andrew, briefly making an exaggerated licking motion into Gemma's folds. His mouth dropped open, lost in desire. Lucas placed himself inside of me.

17

Chapter 17

I exhaled a moan into Gemma's slick folds. Lucas ran his hot palm up my spine to the nape of my neck. Grabbing a fistful of my red curls, I froze. He turned my face toward Andrew's waiting member.

"Service him," his deep voice commanded.

Andrew stepped forward, pressing his thighs into the side of the bed, his cock readied to be taken into my mouth. I positioned my lips at the tip and looked to my god. He nodded his approval and I took Andrew into my mouth, slowly working my lips and tongue down the entirety of his shaft. His eyes were laser beam focused on the sight of my soft pink lips securely positioned around his cock, sliding up and down his length. Lucas positioned himself behind me and pressed deeply inside with a soft grunt.

His steady slow rhythmic stroke picked up in pace and then stopped abruptly. Feeling the cool air rush onto my ass and the back of my thighs, I realized he was no longer behind me. I took my attention from Andrew to look at Lucas. He was behind me—watching me. Lucas stroked his cock with his left hand and rubbed his stomach and chest with the right. His feet shoulder-width apart, eyes glazed over, he continued to pleasure himself. So, I brought my mouth back to Andrew's cock and swallowed him down with everything I had. I rubbed Gemma's glistening swollen clit; she was close again. My loud slurping and sucking did it for Andrew. Feeling his fingers weave themselves into the hair on the back of my head, I slowed down a bit to allow him to push my mouth down the length of his cock.

"Good girl, take it down your throat."

I stopped abruptly and shot him a dirty look.

"I am not your Good Girl."

I spat venom daggers into his face.

"Where do you want this load, slut?"

I glanced at Lucas, still masturbating across the room.

Lucas tucked his chin into his neck. He was trying to restrain himself from orgasm before Andrew. He took in a deep breath.

"Wh-Where," Andrew stuttered.

"Don't," I snapped at him.

Andrew winced and began panting, struggling to stave off his orgasm "You will wait, am I clear?"

Andrew looked to Lucas. Lucas gave no sign of approval or disapproval. He looked back to me and I stared at him expectantly. He nodded, panicked. I grinned a sinister grin and turned to Gemma, licking her juices from the fingers I had inside of her moments earlier. She squirmed and sighed, delighted.

I bit my lower lip and moaned, "Mmm."

And I licked her from between my fingers before sliding them back into her and diving back in for another taste.

Her hands grabbed at my hair wildly; she pulled my face so deep into her waiting pussy that my nose was smashed into her pelvic bone. I exhaled a hot breath into her and she clamped her thighs down in a vice like grip around my ears. Her muffled moans and bucking hips slowed to silence and heavy breathing. She was focusing so she could cum. Her clit felt like a tiny pebble rolling around on my velvet tongue. I felt her walls clamp down on my two fingers. Without warning, Gemma's thighs unhinged themselves from my ears and she shoved her pussy desperately into my nose and mouth once again.

"I-I'm cumming, I'm cumming," she cried out in a high-pitched hoarse voice.

When she finished orgasming, I wiped my mouth with the back of my hand, feeling like a lioness that had taken down her prey, made the kill, and feasted to her heart's content. I was content, smiling, and sweetly caressing Gemma's gorgeous thick thighs. Her head popped up, and she grinned a perfect toothy grin before letting her blonde mane tumble back onto the pillow with a soft 'poof'.

Turning my attention to Lucas, and then back to Andrew, both men had been facing us and watching in awed silence. Ready to be fucked savagely again, I quickly slid off the bed and stood before Andrew, slightly swaying from the intoxication of fucking Gemma, the adrenaline, and the booze coursing through my bloodstream. I took his hand and placed it on my pussy, guiding it up, down, in and out of my folds. I pressed his two fingers into my dripping hole.

"Here."

I breathed into his chin as I stared at Lucas over his shoulder, hoping it would enrage him, and he would tear Andrew's filthy fucking fingers off his property.

He groaned, "You're so wet."

I bit my lip, staring intensely into Lucas' eyes, triple dog daring Lucas with my very best 'fuck me now' sex eyes, to come get what was his. He didn't budge, and this annoyed me.

Tilting my head, I nuzzled his neck and his earlobe before speaking softly, slowly, and seductively into his ear, rubbing his cock and placing his two fingers as far into my pussy as they could go. "

Do you want to fuck me, Andrew?"

His body tensed, his cock twitched and slid up my thigh. I pushed my body into his, moaning softly, writhing against his skin. I was making a scene to get my way.

Andrew turned me around, bending me over the bed. He ripped at the condom foil and tossed the wrapper onto the floor. I heard the pop sound of the final roll of the condom as it was placed all the way on. It was time for Andrew to have me, in front of my god. He didn't stop him. I wanted Lucas to become so possessive and jealous that he couldn't stand it and saved me. I lay there quietly waiting, my face on the bed, cheek pressed into bunched sheets, staring at Lucas staring at Andrew's rubber covered cock, pushing itself into me.

I felt nothing. I mean, I felt him inside me. But there was no pleasure associated with the stimulus. It felt like an alcohol-drenched trip to the gyno's office; clinical—but with panting and grunts emanating from the meat sack with his dick in me. Andrew slapped my right ass cheek. Still nothing. My body and mind were far away, someplace else. Andrew used my body to service himself, pushing it and pulling it, bending my leg if one of my thighs obstructed his access. Striking my flesh, yanking my hair, and I felt numb to the whole lot of things that were happening to me. Lucas' eyes flashed with dark lust, he was riveted and captivated as he watched me being used, pounded, and battered.

Andrew's strokes became furious and erratic, he slipped out a couple of times, bending his dick on my ass cheek, recovering quickly to fuck me like the good little service whore Lucas was training me to be. And I lay there taking it, quietly compliant, until his strokes became halved and quartered, and he shoved his cock as deeply into me as he could, moaning about 'taking it all, whore.' His fluids flooded into the condom. I could feel the heat and the rapid pulsing. His cock lifting and lowering within my walls, once, twice, three times, four times, five, six, seven, a slight twitch on eight and nine, and finally, one last, hard pump on ten, followed by a sated exhale.

He kissed my back once as a thank you for services rendered, before pulling himself out of me. I lay there for a few moments longer feeling nothing, thinking nothing, trying to process but not being able to. Gemma rubbed my hand. I popped my head up and looked at my hand holding tightly to her leg, and then to her face.

"You okay, sweetie?"

I smiled, nodding; feeling the need to reassure her that I was fine. *Don't make anyone uncomfortable, Amber*, I berated myself. I smiled and climbed all the way onto the bed, flopping down beside her with an audible sigh.

"Did you have fun?"

I buried my face in her hair and shoulder, not answering. Lucas made his way over to the side of the bed that I lay sprawled out on. My eyes wandered down his body to his cock. I stared at it lustfully. I wanted so badly to be full of him again. He'd make me better. He was the only one that could. Lucas leaned over and stroked my hair. I leaned my face into the cupped palm of his hand. Kissing his wrist, I made eye contact with him. His eyes were tender and adoring. I melted.

He reached for my hand, pulling me away from Gemma and onto my feet to stand body to body before him. He kissed me deeply.

"You are so fucking sexy, baby."

I melted even further into a puddle of ooze at his feet. I grabbed his cock and began to rub up and down its length.

"Let me make you cum, please. I need to," I spoke into his chin and nipped at his jawline.

He smiled at me and took my hand off his cock. A drop of his pre-cum trailed onto the back of my hand as he pushed my hand down and away–rejecting my advance. I brought my hand to my mouth, making sure he saw his cum glistening in the lamp light.

"You are so fucking sexy, Sir," I said condescendingly, mocking him, as I licked him from my hand.

Lucas's eyes narrowed, searching my face for what exactly I meant.

18

Chapter 18

Lucas tenderly brushed the hair from my cheek.

"You ready to go?" Lucas asked in a hushed tone.

I nodded, yes. He kissed the top of my head and patted my rear end, signaling me to gather our things. We said our goodbyes to Gemma and Andrew, promising to stay in touch, and headed for the truck. He opened the door for me, and I smiled weakly. He smiled back with a slight pout of his lips and softened eyes, which melted my resentment toward him. It was completely unfair how one look from Lucas, one smile, one touch made every wrong fade away. *I'm so fucked*, I mumbled to myself before he climbed in.

I smiled and floated my way through that next week at work. I had been keeping my eye out on other job prospects. With my newfound growing confidence, I felt it was time to no longer be a cocktail waitress. If I was going to be fucked like a grown girl, I needed a job that represented my entrance into *goddesshood*.

That opportunity came calling one particular Thursday afternoon. A position I had applied for with the local tourism and hospitality association was offered to me upon completion of an in-person interview. I interviewed and was hired on the spot. I called up Lucas and shared the incredible news. He expressed his pride in a job well done and insisted we celebrate by meeting a couple he had found for us on the swingers lifestyle site he had signed us up on.

"So, what's their story?" I inquired.

"Well, he is really into your photos, of course. And she is very into women. They want to meet at Schooner's on 3rd South tonight at 8 for drinks and casual talk. If everyone gets along, we will go from there. Stop by my office, and I'll show you their profile."

I smiled into the phone, "I'll be right there."

"Mm... Hurry that sexy ass up," Lucas growled.

My pussy contracted. I bit my lip, smiling and drawing my shoulders up giddily as I ended the call. I shoved the phone into my pocket and headed his way. I pulled into the small parking lot and took a couple of deep breaths as I straightened my long red mane.

"I must be presentable," I mouthed to my reflection in the rearview mirror.

"Amber?" Lucas' voice called out as I opened the front door to his building.

"Tis me," I called back in a poorly executed British accent.

I entered the doorway of the illuminated office to find him sitting back in his chair, legs crossed, sporting a deviant grin. I smiled back broadly. He patted his lap, I came.

Straddling him, I arched my back as his hands ran along my spine, petting my skin and grabbing my curves hungrily. He kissed me deeply, breathing in loudly as his hardening cock pressed into the crotch of my jeans. I adored how turned on he was by my body, how greedy he was, how he just took what he wanted, how he made me want to give more and more of myself to him.

He pulled me away to look at my face.

"Hey there."

And he smiled that tender smile, his eyes soft and adoring. I smiled back and nuzzled his neck.

"Hey yourself."

I ground my soaked pussy into his cock so it was rubbing against my clit. I slid back and forth, torturing myself. I wanted him inside of me.

He sighed and moaned the sexiest deep moan. Lucas removed me from his lap and slammed me down ribs first onto his desk. I stay put while I hear the blessed jingling from the removal of his belt.

"Grab the front of desk, both hands."

He barked his first orders. I did as I was instructed. Lucas unbuttoned and unzipped my jeans pulling them down only to my knees, leaving my black and hot pink thongs in place. He stood behind me in silence, not touching me. I felt the cold air from the a/c licking my shoulders, back, and ass. I lay my head down on my outstretched arms, attempting to see what my god was doing. He was stroking his cock to my lace covered pussy. I felt his hands cup the bottom of my ass cheeks. I stood on my tip toes, shifting from one foot to the other in a desperate effort to align my quaking, hungry pussy, with his cock.

"Please fuck me, now, Sir."

My inner submissive remembered her manners as his rigged hand made hard contact with my left ass cheek. I flung my head back, mouth open, eyes squeezed shut, my red curls stinging my back. I gasped, and my knees went weak. Lucas grabbed my hips and stood me upright forcefully.

"On your toes."

I placed my forehead down onto the desk, taking in a deep breath. Re-centering myself, I rose once again to my tip toes.

"Spread," Lucas commanded through gritted teeth.

So, I scooted my legs as far apart as I could until he stopped me. He ran his fingertips over the crotch of my panties. I began to squirm and shiver. My pussy pulsed and contracted. My clit was thudding and engorged, ready to explode at the slightest flick of the tongue.

"God." I moaned and bit my arm.

"Yes, little girl? What do you want?"

He grabbed my curls, pulling me backward toward him and cooed condescendingly into the fist full of my hair.

My back arched, ass still touching his cock like a good girl, I said in a strained voice, "Inside, inside please."

He let me go, shoving my ribs back down onto his desk. Lucas pulled my panties to the side and pushed deeply into me. We both grunted. Deep and guttural moans escaped our bellies. Me as he crushed my hips and shoulders into the wood and glass of his desk, and him as he pounded into my cervix. He fucked me so good it felt as though my soul were crawling out of my mouth.

19

Chapter 19

"I'm horny," I breathed into the phone one afternoon.

My face was flushed, and the blood couldn't decide which place it needed to be more–in my cheeks and pumping into my racing heart, or to my vagina.

"I'll be there in five minutes," Lucas replied.

Biting my lip, I grinned a devious grin and hung up the phone. His voice was delicious and deep.

Everyone had left the office for the day. The vice-president of the company had entrusted me with the keys to lock up the place when my shift was over. And this is what I was doing with my free rein and trust–I was calling in a favor with my god to fuck me savagely over my desk.

I heard his diesel rumble into the parking lot and my insides squeezed and lurched themselves. Taking a deep breath, I eagerly awaited his presence in the doorway of my office. I was sitting in my chair, dress hugging all the right curves, stilettos on point, prim and proper, back perfectly straight, legs crossed, hair laid with not a strand out-of-place, my hands folded over my thighs, when he poked his head into my office. I flashed my widest smile and he smirked back.

Lucas walked through the doorway and leaned on my desk as he looked around.

"Nice office; much lighter than mine," he nodded toward the large windows across the room. I looked and turned my attention back to him. "Definitely more light."

I laughed, getting up from my chair. I needed to touch him, to have my body pressed firmly into his, and I needed his hand wrapped in my hair, pulling my head so far back I could barely breathe between the tension and the orgasms.

Leaning into him, I wrapped one hand around his waist and nuzzled his neck with my nose and lips. He stood still, allowing me to tease him. His body was warm and rigid, and he smelled faintly of Old Spice, it was never overpowering, it was always just the right mix of him and cologne.

"I was surprised you called; you don't often do that," Lucas said inquisitively.

I smiled into his neck and gave a tiny nibble to provoke him. His body tensed and in one swift movement, I had been twirled around and was now wedged, dress over my hips, legs slightly apart, between Lucas and my desk.

The desk was cutting into my hips. But I remained still and unwavering. He had folded my right hand behind my back and leaned over me so that I was forced to be partially bent over.

"Lie all the way across your desk."

He gave the order, and I followed it. I shoved the pen cup and other bits out-of-the-way and stretched across the top of my desk. He backed off, to the relief of my hip bones. I felt his hands travel over the small of my back, down to my hips where he gave them a hungry squeeze, and then to the bottom of my ass cheeks where he gave them a playful bounce and growled. My pussy clenched hungrily.

He trailed his fingers ever so softly over the crotch of my black panties. I closed my eyes and moaned softly, biting my arm. I felt him tugging them over my hips and down my legs. Lucas knelt behind me and spread my ass and thighs apart, teasing me with his tongue. My mind exploded into brilliant bursts of colors that melded one into the other. I felt myself slipping into that warm fuzzy place as my eyes rolled around in their sockets. I was losing grip; and then-

"I need you," I blurted out.

Lucas froze, and so did I.

I crash landed back into a very bleak and harsh reality. No more fuzzy warm place for me, probably ever again. I didn't dare breathe, or blink, or think. I just listened and let what had tumbled out of my mouth hang in the air, while he decided what to do with it.

Shit, shit, fuck! Stupid, stupid. What the fuck did you just do, Amber? My thoughts raced and now my face was flushed for an entirely different reason. Lucas stood from his position behind me. So, I lifted myself, adjusting and straightening while mentally preparing for the dismissal. I turned to face him, looking down at the floor. He touched my chin and gently pulled my face upward so that our eyes met. I looked down again. I was so ashamed and upset with myself for making him uncomfortable.

"Look at me," he commanded softly.

My eyes trailed up his body until landing on his honey eyes.

"I'm sorry. I-I wasn't thinking," I blathered. My eyes misted over, "It won't happen again. I know what you said."

I referred to the day in the truck when he had told me to not fall in love with him. He stared intently, studying my face. And then, he pressed his lips tenderly against mine. Stunned, I stood there, my arms, two heavy bricks at my side. I let him kiss my mouth as a single tear rolled down my left cheek.

Pulling back from the kiss, Lucas looked at me with a profound tenderness that I was not used to from him. It threw my senses into chaos. He pushed a stray pen out of the way, clearing a space for what I was assuming me, on my desk.

"Sit down, and then slowly lie back, slowly, do you understand?" He spoke softly.

"Yes, Sir."

Caressing my face before I lay back as ordered, he ran his hand through my hair and pulled my face close, whispering in my ear, "That's my good girl."

I melted…

Lucas breathed me in and gently pushed me down. He knelt before me, and buried his face in my pussy, his tongue bringing me in and out of delirium. Yet, another gift—yet another orgasm. My body heaved, and my back arched off the desk. I grabbed at the corners to find something solid to hold onto because I was 100% certain that I was going to float away. But I couldn't find them. I managed to grab a handful of pens and tossed them down before smacking the wood with the palm of my hand as he bit down on my clit.

I cried out, slamming my thighs closed, holding his head hostage in a vice like grip. Pulling at his hair, I attempted to move in the opposite direction of his face, only to find myself grinding my pussy right back into his mouth when I felt the warmth of his tongue sliding expertly over my hurt feelings once again. Forgiven, my thighs relaxed, and I took a few deep breaths.

"I-Luc…" I moaned, attempting a sentence. "Luc-Lucas."

I ran my fingers through his hair to get his attention. He moaned and exhaled into my folds. My eyes rolled into another dimension. No more thoughts, only feels. I surrendered to it. I surrendered to him.

I felt it rising; bubbling up, a slow drumming, fading in rather than out. And before I knew it, the orgasm was upon me. I tapped Lucas' shoulder and squeezed because no words would come out. It felt like I had birthed this fucking orgasm.

I screamed, "FUCK!"

My back arched off the desktop like something from the exorcist and if it weren't for my hands holding the top of my head, I am certain it would have spun 360 degrees.

20

Chapter 20

Lucas held me in place until he had sucked every drop of orgasm from my body. I touched his head and shimmied away slightly to signify that I was absolutely sated. He stood, slowly drawing his forearm across his lips. The look in his eyes declared war; a war I was no stranger to. So, I mentally prepared myself to become his enemy. We weren't on the same team anymore, and perhaps, we never had been. Perhaps, we never would be. Perhaps, my body and mind were his bloody battleground. If, in this moment, I have captured what it feels like to meet one's maker then, perhaps, I wish to never agree with this god.

May there be eternal discord in all of the land, so mote it be. When finished with my request to the universe, I mentally drug my foot across the hypothetical line in the sand in a bratty attempt to muddy it all. There are no lines that I wouldn't allow him to cross, as I am his and he can have whatever the fuck he wants.

Game on.

We stared into one another's eyes for what seemed like an eternity. Me, half not knowing what position to assume so that he may invade at his pleasure and half being so turned on I couldn't stand myself because of the suspense. He was no doubt plotting his hostile takeover. I scooted to the edge of my desk until my feet were able to touch the floor. Standing unsteadily, I could feel my insides still convulsing and pulsing lightly. I was a mess down there and best case scenario, he was about to make it worse.

Something in the silence made my stomach wrench. *Usually, he has stated what he wants me to do by now,* I thought nervously. His eyes roamed my body lustfully. He pointed his right pointer finger in the air and made a circular motion. Severely confused by this, my face twisted into a perplexed grimace and my head recoiled.

"Undress-now," he finally spoke. His tone was tender yet firm.

I immediately slid my dress over my head, allowing it to fall from my hand to the floor. Leaning down to take off my heels, his voice blasted through me.

"Leave them on."

So, I did, and I stood, my back straight as a board, allowing my hands to fall softly at my sides, palms upward, exposing my body for his viewing pleasure.

Lucas' eyes continued to explore my body. The courage I had began to subside as the endorphins from the orgasm that had intoxicated me moments ago, brought me crashing back into reality. He was examining my body from across the room; like, really closely examining me. I felt every inch of me begin to tingle. It was almost as if his eyes were tentacles reaching out and brushing my skin with every glance. Making direct eye contact with me, Lucas pointed his right index and middle finger downward at the floor and shook them slightly in what seemed to me a come hither signal and nodded his chin toward the floor at his side. He never took his eyes off mine. I had allowed my attention to travel down the length of his delicious thick fingers. Biting my lip, letting it slide slowly from between my teeth as my gaze met his once again, I allowed my jaw to hang slightly ajar.

He shook his fingers toward the floor once more. Slowly, I knelt on the carpet, searching his eyes for a sign that he was pleased and that I was his good girl. He raised his chin as his gaze followed my body to the floor. As he looked down upon me, I could tell he was in his element. I was triggering his monster. His fingers fixed, pointed toward the floor still, he shook them once more.

"Come to me," he said softly.

I stared into his eyes, searching them for the meaning behind this moment. There was something-something that I couldn't quite put my finger on to name it but- something significant was happening here. It was in the air, a palpable heartbeat in the chest of this beast of a moment. My head screamed to question him and everything about this situation out of curiosity, while my heart, feeling the beauty of this surrender as deeply as ever, crumbled and caved in on itself.

I placed my hands on the floor, lowered my eyes, and crawled to him.

When I reached his hand, I sat back on my knees. My eyes still lowered, I secretly craved to take his strong fingers into my mouth. I could feel the tingling and pulsating sensations between my legs at the thought. I could no longer stand not touching Lucas anymore, so I reached up to touch his hand.

"No," he barked.

I jumped at the sharpness in his tone and quickly placed my hands at my sides on the floor.

"I-I'm sorry, I just-" I began to stutter.

My mind had just been scrambled by one word from him.

Lucas grabbed a handful of my hair and pulled my head back, exposing my neck and breasts. Holding me there, he bent down to look into my eyes. I shut them. I didn't know why, but I shut them. I couldn't bear to look at him. I felt some fear, and it surged through my veins like little electrical currents, zapping me in all the right ways, in all the right places. I felt myself getting wetter as I shuffled to not topple over.

"Did I tell you to speak, Amber?"

Lucas' breath was warm on my cheek. I shook my head, no.

"Open your eyes and look at me," he commanded.

I opened my eyes and stared up at him. My vision was crystal clear. It was as if I was peering through eyes that weren't my own. I felt present and replaced all at the same time. I took a deep breath in and held it. Lucas' grip tightened on my hair and he placed his mouth just to the left corner of mine.

"Did I tell you that you could touch me, Amber?"

I squeezed my eyes shut and shook my head, no.

"You know what happens to disobedient little girls, young lady?" he growled, his jaw tensed.

I heard him swallow. My mouth was dry from breathing in through it. I shook my head no once again. Lucas stood, taking me with him by my hair. My eyes popped open, and I grabbed the hand holding my hair. Wincing in pain, I felt panic setting in. I wasn't sure what happened to bad girls in Lucas' world, exactly. I had flashes of the hotel bathroom; my head being slammed into the wall, Lucas' spit landing on my lip, me licking it off, and my face smearing up and down inside the white porcelain sink as he fucked me savagely.

If that is what happened to disobedient little girls, then perhaps it would be well worth it to misbehave more often. I danced back and forth between panic and delight for a few brief moments until deciding to stay completely still and obedient. Taking a few deep breaths, I made a conscious effort to calm my mind. In the meantime, Lucas was unbuckling his belt while holding my face against the floor to ceiling window that overlooked the parking lot of my building. I heard his belt slide off in one swoop from his dress slacks, the buckle jingling as it hung in his hand.

All at once, he was no longer touching me and the heat that had been radiating into my back side was replaced with a cool draft of air. I kept my body pressed against the warmed panel of glass. I saw two employees in different suites exiting their building doors and walking toward their cars. My breath was fogging up a small patch of glass and the moisture was making my face damp around my nostrils and mouth. Pressing my forehead against the window, I waged war against my curiosity to see what Lucas was doing behind me.

His silence was disconcerting, and he was behaving in ways that I hadn't yet seen. The hand signals, the silence, the aggression- *What is happening?* I pondered. And then, his voice-deep and deviant, shattered the tension.

"Are you mine, little girl?"

My eyes darted toward my right shoulder. Turning to face him, I slowly walked to where he stood, leaning on the corner of my desk. I turned my back to him, pressing my body into his, reveling in his warmth. I placed his right hand over my throat and his hallowed left hand on my pussy, working his fingers inside of me.

"I am yours, Sir." I moaned, snaking my body in every which way to make sure Lucas had access to push deep inside of me. My knees buckled from the pleasure, as his fingers worked my pussy expertly, as only he could.

"Let me... please you," I breathed into Lucas' collar bone, rubbing him through his slacks.

I took the belt from his hand and placed it around my neck, cinching it just tight enough to press into my throat slightly, and I handed him the other end. He was fully aroused and made no fuss about me taking him from his pants. Looking into his eyes, I knelt down and took him into my mouth. The belt smelled of his cologne and leather, it was an intoxicating combination—both the smell and the feeling. The metal was warming against my trachea. With every inch of him I took into my mouth, the corner of the buckle pushed into me, triggering my gag reflex and my ever growing submissive nature.

Turning my head, I began to cough. Lucas allowed me one deep breath in before yanking the belt, forcing my face back onto his waiting cock. My stomach was in knots and I felt like I was going to throw up. My throat contracted in response to his member sliding beyond my tonsils. My back arched outward and I placed my hands on his thighs to pull away before I puked. He held the belt taught and grabbed the back of my head, holding it firmly in place. I had every inch of him down my throat and began to drool, as I could not swallow.

Lucas groaned, letting me go, and thrust in once more. His thighs tensed and shook, and his right hand, trembling frantically, grabbed at the back of my head to hold it in place again.

"Just like that," Lucas growled.

His desperation for release screamed at me. So, I kept it, just like that. He pushed into my mouth is short strokes, so that the head of his cock rubbed the very back of my throat. I felt his cock harden even more and begin throbbing. His cum streamed in spurts down my throat. I swallowed him down and sucked the head of his cock before allowing him to fully leave my mouth. I wanted to be sure he had fully released, not wanting to miss a single drop of his orgasm.

He released me and leaned into my desk. I wiped my mouth and stood slowly, steadying myself. The adrenaline was coursing through me again and I could feel a stream of my own running down my inner thighs. He kissed my forehead and took the belt from around my neck. I closed my eyes and enjoyed the tenderness of the moment. I felt satisfied and accomplished. We both straightened our disheveled selves, dressing in silence. Lucas promised to text me later and left. I headed for home shortly after, making sure everything was perfectly back in place and praying that no one had heard or seen any of the commotion that had just occurred.

21

Chapter 21

8 PM- I was settling into bed with a book when my phone buzzed. It reminded me to turn the sound back on so that I would hear my alarm in the morning. Picking it up, I saw Lucas' name and a preview of his text.

Lucas: Multimedia Message-Dinner and drinks tomorrow with-

I opened the message, so I could see it in its entirety.

Lucas: Dinner and drinks tomorrow with Garrett and Kat, be ready by 6 PM?

I carefully studied the photo. Garrett was a strapping older gentleman; he looked to be in his forties, a boyish smile that I found so enticing I began smiling along with him. He was handsome, stocky-possibly military, from what I could see. Kat had blue eyes and shoulder length curly blonde hair. She was tan, maybe around the same age as Garrett. And they were squished into the photo together, arms around one another's backs. Just as I was about to dig into the interpretation of their body language in the photo, my phone buzzed again, and again, and again.

Lucas had texted me three more photos. Opening the first one, I nearly dropped my phone. It was an up-close picture of Kat's breasts.

"Wow..." I mumbled under my breath.

The next picture was Garrett plowing into Kat something fierce.

"Double wow..." I gawked.

Picture three: Kat being mauled by two other men, neither of which looked like Garrett.

"Oh!" I said aloud, covering my mouth.

My eyebrows were raised as high as they could possibly go, and my eyes felt as if they were going to bug out of their sockets. I could hear myself breathing as I scrolled through the photos time and again, and it reminded me to close my mouth. My jaw had been hanging agape for several minutes.

The photos were shocking to say the least. Shocking yet intriguing. I wanted to know more. So, I sent a reply back to Lucas.

Me: 6 PM tomorrow, I'll be ready.

He sent back a wink face and I smiled at my phone like a schoolgirl that had just gotten her first kiss. I adored our adventures. I adored his body heaving itself into mine. I adored how he made my body sing and my mind think. I was his and he was mine, even if he didn't know it—even if he didn't want to be—it was so. Scrolling through the photos of Garrett and Kat, I felt my cheeks begin to flush. I was drawn to the one picture of Kat and the two men. She was on her back in what looked to be a hotel room bed, her eyes fixed on the man's face that had himself firmly planted, hips deep, down her throat. Her calves were draped over the other man's muscular arms, his hands gripping her thighs, pulling her into him. The photo cast her as a rag doll of sorts; a rag doll made of flesh and bone that had been tossed into a lion's den, and she was being made a meal of.

I plugged my phone in for the evening and headed for the shower. It felt incredible to wash off the day. As I splashed the water over my body and felt it trickle over my vagina, my fingers wove their way into my folds. I was incredibly wet. The photos must have turned me on more than I realized. I leaned against the shower wall and allowed my right hand to grip my breasts while my left hand sought out and found my slightly swollen clit. At the slightest touch, it sent waves of longing and pleasure through my entire body. My knees weakened so I steadied myself and continued.

Closing my eyes, I could see the image of Garrett pushing forcefully into Kat from behind. His back arched inward, her back arched downward. Both of their heads were thrown back, her mouth open, his jaw clenched. Such a different beast from the man with the boyish smile in the first photo Lucas had sent to me. It made me curious, it made me horny as hell. I couldn't quite explain my excitement to meet Garrett and Kat. I also couldn't quite put my finger on why or how it was that I had found myself in my shower, about to cum to a strange man and his wife's sex pictures and not Lucas.

We had been with some couples- and they were fun. They piqued my curiosity. But there was something inherently magnetic about Garrett... seductive. And by proxy, I must go through Kat to get to him. I was already strategizing. I didn't want to steal him away. I just wanted my way with him. I wanted to find out why I was so drawn to him, why his smile made me smile. *Tomorrow...* I told myself as I rolled my fingertips around my clit, pushing myself over the edge and into intense orgasm.

"Fuck, mmm-" I whimpered, biting my bottom lip in an attempt to keep quiet.

My body quaked, arched, and began sliding down the shower wall. I ended up on my knees in the tub with the shower spraying on my head and back. I rested my forearms on the side of the tub and lay my head atop them, panting and shivering from the endorphins coursing through my system. A chill had curled itself around my spine, tickling my insides outward and my entire body responded by lurching itself at odd angles for a few seconds. And then, the quiet came... It was just the streaming water and me. The water seemed so loud. Perhaps amplified by the tub walls, perhaps amplified by my heightened senses, post orgasm. My thoughts flitted here and there as the convulsing in my pussy rescinded.

For reasons unbeknownst to me, I began to feel a sense of shame—it felt kind of dirty and beneath me to be masturbating to other people's pictures in the shower. I felt guilty for desiring someone other than Lucas. I was entering the grey area. I was spinning, and I needed hands around my throat. My pussy contracted and began throbbing as I placed my own hands around my neck for what comfort I could find. I applied some pressure; but it wasn't Lucas' hands. It didn't have quite the same affect. So, I took my hands from my throat and stood up, washed my hair and body, dried off, dressed, and slipped under the covers. Lying there in the dark, my mind wandered to tomorrow's dinner, Garrett, Kat, Lucas, and the fucking I intended to push for. I needed to get my head clear and the only thing that seemed to help was hands around my throat and a superb fucking; I needed to be demolished.

So, I fucked myself enough to blot out the guilt and shame, I came again, just not as intensely as before. *I'm so fucked up*, I criticize myself, feeling shame. I thought of Lucas' glazed over eyes, his hand slowly stroking his cock to my body and felt better, my pussy contracted. I was strung-out—like an addict—all the sex in the world would never be enough, and I was coming to terms with this knowledge. Booze and Lucas, they were my Band-Aid.

22

Chapter 22

The work day passed quickly. My head was in the clouds for the better part of it. Tantalizing images of what could be in store for me later danced in my head, tickling my frontal lobes and certain areas that were, sadly, still neatly tucked away in my burgundy lace panties. I spritzed on my favorite Jasmine and Orange Blossom perfume and smiled. Tonight, I had a feeling about fond feelings; about, warm, fuzzy, sexy, naughty feelings.

Lucas' text came through, bringing a devious smile to my lips. He was outside waiting. I gave one last lick to my teeth in the mirror—perfection. Tossing a very brief, "I'll be back later tonight," at my mother, I scampered out the door and literally bounced into his vehicle. I shut the door and looked over at Lucas, smiling my widest grin. He smiled a sideways smile back at me through the sexiest pout I had ever had the very stimulating pleasure of bearing witness to. "Seatbelt," he reminded me gently. I felt all warm and squirmy inside instantaneously.

The varying range of emotions that demanded they all be felt at once was overwhelming and glorious. Tonight was magical for a number of personal reasons, and a number of reasons I am certain even Lucas wasn't aware of. But that was going to have to be okay because, this time, I wanted what I wanted for me.

Twenty minutes later, we walked into the restaurant and were led to the patio where Kat and Garrett sat, awaiting our arrival. This bull of a man stood and straightened his shirt as we approached. Our eyes found one another immediately. I floated the rest of the way toward them with Lucas' hand firmly in the small of my back, guiding me. The two men shook hands and politely nodded at one another, exchanging their formal greetings. Lucas introduced himself and then me.

I leaned in and gave Kat a one armed hug. And then, it was Garrett's turn; he met me halfway around the table and took me into his strong arms, squeezing me perfectly. Pulling back from his embrace, we looked briefly into one another's eyes—I felt my face turning red. I knew there was something about this man, and I knew he felt it too; the energy, the connection, the unspoken sexual tension.

Lucas pulled the chair out for me and I sat as he scooted me in. Smiling at how much of a gentleman he was being, I leaned into his kiss on my forehead and closed my eyes. He looked at me adoringly and I reveled in it. It didn't happen often, this tenderness. So, I lapped it up like a kitten with a bowl of warm milk before her. Kat and Garrett smiled at the loving display and looked at each other before abruptly and simultaneously taking a sip from their cocktails. I could've sworn I picked up on some stressful tension between the pair, but I wasn't entirely sure what I had seen. I decided to dismiss the gut feeling I had that something was off between them.

The drinks flowed, as did the sparks across the table between Lucas and Kat. Garrett and I did our best to pay equal amounts of attention to our partners but the draw to one another was magnetic. Somewhere amidst my third margarita, I kissed Lucas on the lips and whispered that I was going to move over a seat to sit by Garrett. He nodded his approval and kissed me again. I moved across the table and he scooted in close to Kat. They had been making eyes all evening and I knew she was very into Lucas. Sitting next to Garrett, my soul exhaled, *Finally.* A warm tropical breeze blew strands of hair across my face and some of it got caught in my lipstick. Garrett brushed it away with an adoring smile on his face.

I felt my face growing hot again. Returning his smile, I tucked my hair behind my ears and made a remark about pulling my hair up to keep it out of my makeup. He adamantly disagreed, saying how gorgeous I was with my hair down and that my hair was stunning.

"You smell incredible. What are you wearing?"

Once again, I was smiling like a schoolgirl all in my bliss. Boldly, I pulled my red mane over my right shoulder, so he could catch a closer whiff of my neck. Leaning in to allow him access, I leaned my head to the right, exposing my collar bone to him.

"It is a Jasmine and Orange Blossom fragrance," I said, brushing my lips across his temple while I spoke.

He nuzzled my neck discreetly on his way up.

"It is intoxicating, or perhaps, it's just you that makes this perfume intoxicating?"

We stared into one another's eyes, caught up in yet another intense moment, the both of us, wishing with every fiber of our beings that we were already tangled up in the other.

A smile formed at the corner of my mouth. I picked up my drink to break the tension and Garrett followed suit. Making eye contact with Lucas as I drank down the last of my drink, his eyes were dark brown and stormy. I could tell Kat and the Gin and tonics were bringing out the animal in him. She was going to be in for quite a treat later, little did she know. But I knew. I could see his primal side gnashing its teeth behind those gorgeous, dark and impossibly long lashes.

I felt my pussy contract, so I shifted in my seat, uncrossing and crossing my legs the other way. The waitress arrived with another round of drinks. She distributed them, breaking the tense silence that had fallen over the table. I smiled politely at Kat, who was clearly very intoxicated already.

She smiled broadly at me and slurred, "You're so pretty. Garrett really likes–you…"

Garrett looked over at his wife with a look of dismay.

"Isn't she so pretty, baby?"

Kat pawed at his jaw to make him look at me.

"She is lovely," Garrett replied quietly.

He looked at me apologetically. I smiled an understanding smile. Kat caught the exchange between him and me and stared directly into my eyes, slightly squinting as if she were trying to decipher just exactly what in the fuck was going on.

She turned her attention suddenly to Lucas. They looked as deeply into one another's eyes as two highly intoxicated people could.

"You are- very lucky man, and so sexy. You two are married, yes?" Kat inquired, sipping at her drink.

Lucas chimed in quickly, "No. We are just swing partners."

I shot him a look of disbelief. He looked back at me with no discernable facial gestures, simply blank… His words cut me deeply, reminding me of how little I meant to him in reality. I didn't expect him to say we were married, but I didn't expect him to offer so quickly a correction to her question, much less saying that we were "just" swing partners. The truth of our actuality was a sharp slap in the face.

I felt myself retreat inside myself. My heart was shattered. I knew better; he had told me to not fall in love with him. But I couldn't fucking help myself. It didn't help matters and that he ate my attention, and sickening displays of subservience to him up like a fucking glutton, but so was I. I was probably worse than he was.

I realized that the moment had become uncomfortable for everyone at the table and I immediately felt ashamed for having displayed any discernible emotion and that it would make Lucas appear to be an asshole for upsetting me, so I smiled-reassuring everyone that all was well. The awkwardness began to dissipate.

We all finished up our last drinks and decided to head back to their hotel room. Garrett pulled my chair out for me and Lucas helped Kat out of hers.

She placed her hand on his chest, smiled up at him, and slurred into his shoulder, "Such a gentleman."

He smiled down at her a deviant smile and they locked eyes for a moment–fucking one another mentally. I knew that look well, on behalf of other women, as me being one myself, and on behalf of Lucas, as he has fucked me with his eyes a million times. Being more sensitive because of what had happened earlier, I felt a sense of jealousy washing over me.

My resolve to fuck the ever-living shit out of Garrett upgraded to a category five. I walked silently by his side, storms raging in my spirit, and being sure to not make any physical contact with him all of the way to Kat and Garrett's hotel room. If he touched me, all would be forgiven. I didn't want to forgive him–just yet. I knew he knew I was angry with him. He didn't attempt to touch me or speak to me. We all made small talk once inside the room. Lucas grabbed me by elbow and pulled me in for a kiss finally. For the first time, I felt my heartbreaking and my guts twisting as his lips cooled from the beer he was sipping on pressed into mine. I wanted to be angry with him and there was nothing he was going to do to change that. I allowed him to kiss me and pulled away as the kiss came to a close. I looked down at the floor because I couldn't stand to look at his face. I'd cave.

I was weak and we both knew it. He pulled my chin up to make me look at him.

"You okay?"

He nodded what my appropriate response should be. I looked deeply into his eyes, and mustered a polite smile, nodding, Yes. I looked away guiltily; I was totally lying. He knew I was lying as well, because his eyes followed mine as they fell to the ground. He took his hands off me and went for his beer, chugging it and setting it down with a glass thud.

Turning his attention to Kat, who was already panty-less on the bed and spread eagle, her pussy awaiting a hard cock pumping into it mercilessly, Lucas adjusted his stiffening member before undressing himself and crawling onto the bed, mounting her. I stood a foot away from the end of the fold out couch bed, watching this clusterfuck of the two of them drunkenly mauling one another. For the first time, I wasn't in the least turned on by this display. I felt nothing but sympathy—maybe a bit for myself and a bit for the two of them. *How sad it must be to have to wake up and go to sleep as him or as her*, I thought, feeling myself becoming angry again.

I needed to fuck to make it go away; the thoughts, the hurt, the sadness…Garrett was standing at the side of the bed, watching his wife get fucked by Lucas and observing me, observing them. When we made eye contact, his face expressed concern and desire all at once. Red Light, Green Light—Green light.

I peeled my shirt off—never taking my eyes off him. His eyes darkened as desire raked her nails down his spine. His chest and shoulders squared as if he were readying himself to body slam me onto the bed aside his howling wife. I came out of my bra and watched his lungs fill to the brim with his silent gasp. I was pleased with this reaction, so I slid out of my jeans and walked over to the bed, lying on my back. He walked to the edge of the bed where I lay and stood: a vision of sex, desire, and masculinity. I spread my legs open and began running my fingers over my pussy through my mauve colored satin panties.

Garrett reached out and stroked my ankle with the back of his right hand. I bit my lip and pulled my panties to the side, giving him a peek of what was behind the thin veil preventing his cock from being deep inside of me. He licked his lips and smiled that boyish smile I had seen in his photo- the one that made me beam myself. Only, this time, I was able to return that grin to him. There he stood, over me, us both grinning at one another like fools. I giggled, and he pounced on me. Lucas and Kat were in the throes of drunken passion. He looked over at me, that familiar glazed over stare ensued while he pounded away at her cervix. Garrett was kissing and nibbling at the right side of my neck. Lucas' and my eyes remained locked. I bit my lip and squirmed beneath Garrett, moaning softly. As I ran my nails up his back and over his shoulders, I closed my eyes—disconnecting from my god. I slipped into blackness—a blackness so deep and dark I couldn't feel the bed below me or the body on top of me, just feather light strokes that felt like silk sheets sliding off my naked skin, and the occasional sharp stinging pain of his teeth gripping my skin. It was absolute bliss.

I writhed beneath Garrett's solid body. I tried to grab at his flesh to pull him into me, but it was to no avail—he was all stone and sweat. The air in the room was thick and hard to breathe; far too much panting happening and not enough fresh air to go around. His body untangled itself from mine, and I came down from my floaty black space, opening my eyes. Garrett's butterscotch eyes looked deeply into mine as he raised my left leg, kissing and nibbling at my calf, gauging my response, and then my knee, gauging my response, and then my lower thigh, he licked his lips and a sly smile formed at the right corner of his mouth. My pussy contracted. She was a bottomless pit, a man eater, a people pleaser, a greedy-starving bitch, hell bent on getting what she wanted by any means necessary.

I knew this about myself and was becoming the person whose personal philosophy in life was, 'If you can't beat 'em, join 'em.' There is no conquering her unless she lets you. And I had no desire to conquer her. She knew what was best—what I needed to feel okay in my skin for a few days and who was I to question that? So, I didn't; I gave her what she wanted; all of the boys and the girls. Right now, she wanted this bull of a boy's chest heaving itself onto my body. She wanted his breath on my neck and in my ear, she wanted him so deep inside of her one wouldn't be able to tell where she began, and he ended. She wanted to hear his moans. She wanted them all. She wanted him to herself—just for now.

23

Chapter 23

Lucas grabbed my hair pulling me toward him abruptly. I winced, and my hand shot up to lessen the tension automatically.

"Suck her off my cock."

He pulled out of Kat and turned his member toward me. Garrett moved back to allow me enough freedom to attend to him. Rolling over, I crawled to him. I began by running my tongue up the length of the bottom of him. I looked him in his eyes and saw that it was good, so I proceeded with a long lick up each side, swirling my tongue around the head. His low deep groans made my pussy throb. She was ready to eat—she demanded to be filled.

I opened my mouth wide and took him fully in. He held my head in place, growling.

"Fuck! That's my good girl. You want this cum?"

I began to gag. He held my head in place for a few more seconds while my body heaved. I placed my hand on his right thigh. He let go. My head dropped, his cock tangling in my hair as I gagged and dry heaved. I felt the alcohol rise into my throat, so I tried breathing deeply to keep it all down. It stayed down, and I placed him back in my mouth. Lucas' hips swayed back and forth, pumping himself in measured strokes in and out of my lips, just the head sliding over my tongue rapidly. Garrett had climbed atop his wife, he had her by the throat with one hand and slapped her breasts with the other as he pushed into her.

"You want this cock, you fucking slut?"

Kat howled unintelligible words.

Lucas pulled himself from my mouth to go grab his beer. I lay on my back, watching Garrett massacre Kat. I was shocked by how different he was with her. With me, he had been so sensual and passionate. With her, he was rough and demeaning. The severe contrast in his sexual natures both intrigued and turned me on. I was erring more on the side of intrigued, though. There was no way I could ever stand for anyone to slap my breasts or twist and pull them the way he has with her.

Lucas came back, lounging on the bed beside me, watching the two of them. Garrett flipped Kat over and began fucking her hard and fast. He slapped her ass with a loud sharp 'TWACK'. Kat's back arched deeply inward and she bit the pillow. By this point, she was making no noise, and she was holding her breath in with a mouth full of pillow. Her body was completely tense and stationed. She was about to have one hell of an orgasm. I knew that stance. Good job, Garrett; well done. He grabbed two handfuls of her ass, pulling her wide-open and drilled into her again and again. Kat screamed into the pillow, her body shaking violently. Lucas began rubbing his cock unconsciously. Admittedly, it was fucking hot.

Garrett pushed violently into her one last time and held himself there. Every inch of him was firmly planted within her. She whimpered, and her body collapsed, completely sated and exhausted.

"I think she needs my cock in her mouth," Lucas growled into my ear.

I bit my lip and smiled, nodding my approval. He kissed my forehead and rose from the bed.

Everyone took a brief bathroom break and the air conditioner was turned on. Garrett and I were the first ones back to the bed. We sat momentarily in silence, entirely nude, drinking bottled water and trying to cool off. I could feel the sweat starting to dry on my body and began to feel a bit chilly.

"Are you having a good time?" Garrett inquired.

I nodded as I brought the bottle to my lips, swallowing with a loud gulp, or it seemed loud to me. The bottle popped back into shape, making me jump. Garrett didn't respond, I am not sure he noticed. He just touched my pinkie knuckle with his index finger knuckle. I was staring at my toes when he touched my hand. My eyes darted to his hand; his thick-strong hand. I heard Kat's gasping echoing in my mind and reminisced about earlier when he was strangling her and calling her a slut. Brief, seconds' long flashes of Garrett engaging with his wife ping ponged about in my brain, displaying themselves like fireworks behind my eyes; lighting me up from the inside out. I thought I might like to be called a slut. I can be a slut and a good girl too.

"Do you want this cock, you fucking slut?" His words to Kat echoed throughout my being. It made my pussy throb and beg. "Yes, please..." She purred. I shifted and resettled, taking a deep breath and another gulp of my water. Lucas and Kat reappeared, breaking the moment that Garrett and I were sharing. We both jumped back into, *Lights, Camera, Action.*

Nothing to see here... We have done nothing wrong. Yet, I felt guilty and my cheeks began to flush in the starched glow of the bathroom lights. I poured myself a shot from the bottle of tequila they had brought and downed it before turning to face Lucas and smile as I tucked my nose and forehead into his chest. I felt much more myself as the liquor rushed into my bloodstream. It turned down my feelings and turned up my sex. Emboldened by the alcohol, which had fully integrated itself into my system by then, I kissed Lucas deeply and then turned my back to him, tucking myself into his body. I wrapped his arms around my figure and trailed his left hand down my abdomen and to my pussy while Kat and Garrett watched. Lucas allowed it. He was all in his bliss as I slipped his fingers into my folds. I felt him take control as he pushed my head to the side, exposing my neck to him.

I stared straight ahead at Garrett, who didn't have the same glazed-over sex eyes that Lucas and the others had when they saw me approaching my glory. His eyes were aware, awake, burning, and absolutely seeing me—not past me. He was present. I wanted him to taste me. I wanted to taste him. Taking Lucas' fingers from my pussy after a few moments, I brought them to my mouth and licked them clean. I felt his chest grumble as a soft growl rolled its way up to his throat. He breathed a hot exhale into my ear. My eyes rolled into the back of my head and my knees weakened. I pushed my ass into his hips and felt his desire for me.

That's it, I will have him to myself. I need, I want, I must. So, I went to Kat, who was lying on the bed, spread eagle, playing with her shaven pussy, and I stood by the bedside watching her. Lightly, I traced my fingers over her lips below, and she pushed her hips forward, urging me to touch her more. Climbing onto the bed, I pushed my fingers into her, slowly at first. She began to buck her hips as I curled my index and middle fingers into a 'come hither' motion, stroking her G-spot. Her moans turned to howls with every stroke that met and matched her rhythm. I stopped fucking her abruptly. She untangled her face from the pillow, her head flying up, mouth open in silent protest. I shot her a devious look and rose from between her legs to attend to her husband.

Giving one last glance back toward Lucas, I smiled, drank down the last of the liquor in my cup, and headed toward Garrett. I leaned in to whisper to him that I wanted to be alone with him, but he beat me to it.

"Let's go into the other room, I'd like to have some privacy with you."

I smiled broadly into his amazing jaw line.

"You took the words right out of my mouth," I cooed back.

We beamed at one another knowingly. There was that something magical between us that couldn't be justly dignified with words. So, we used our smiles and our eyes, and our sex until the words came—or until we did.

24

Chapter 24

I pulled my panties back over my bottom—for the sole purpose of Garrett having something to take off of me. I led him into the 'study' part of their hotel suite, pushed him down onto the sofa playfully, and straddled him. Finally, I had him where I wanted him, and now, I was going to eat him. I ground my sex into his and placed his hands on my 36DD's. He happily obliged me by taking them one after the other into his warm mouth, sucking and licking seductively. My breasts weren't necessarily as sensitive as I had witnessed some women's, but I derived great pleasure from the act of worship. My hands automatically went to his hair, running my fingers through the sides and then over the top of his head and to the back, where I leaned over, placing my face by his ear, cradling him and rocking while nibbling his earlobe.

He was in my cocoon, under my spell, perfectly in his bliss and I was determined to make this one burst open and fly into the sky, phoenix style. I wanted to hear his war cry. *Let's do battle*, my eyes, hypodermic needles, injecting my greatest desire in that moment into his bloodstream, so that mine became his, circulating, until running its course or he received another dose of me.

He grabbed my face and pressed his lips to mine, we were both panting into one another's mouths like emaciated wolves showing their teeth and ripping away at the flesh and bones of their first kill in ages. He poured into a void that I didn't realize existed; and between it and the tequila, they made me vicious. Garrett was my first chance at nourishment in way too long. Judging from the handful of crotch I was gripping possessively, and his feverish fits of moans into my mouth, I'd venture to say he was just as hungry as I was.

So, here we go.

"F-floor. Floor. I want you-floor," Garrett spat out and pointed downward, caveman style.

I nodded fervently in agreement and allowed him to lift me off him, holding me securely to ensure I did not fall over or trip. I caught that, and it sucker punched my raging libido just hard enough to bring my lust to a dull roar. Tender... He seemed so sweet. I thought back to the look of disdain between him and Kat at the dinner table earlier. I was confused as to how there would be any trouble in paradise with this one, at least the bad kind of trouble. My inner demons shrugged their shoulders and dismissed my thoughts to recess.

It's time to play, the blackest of my depths screeched.

Garrett pulled me down onto him. I fell forward hard and knocked some of the wind out of him. We both giggled, and I apologized, checking to ensure that he was relatively unharmed. He assured me that all was well, and his face grew somber. Touching my cheek with his fingers as tenderly as I had ever been touched by any man, he stroked my face. His eyes traveled my features, finally resting on mine. He grabbed my chin, holding it in place.

"You are remarkably beautiful."

My mouth became dry and I realized I was still as a church mouse, my jaw hanging open–a literal mouth breather moment. I don't know how long it had been since I had blinked, or swallowed, or moved, for that matter. In this space, I knew nothing of time or its origins. It was not relative; fuck time and fuck sensibility, I was in a trance. My brain couldn't human. If this was 'awe', I was most certainly in it, on it, and of it.

"You okay, baby?"

I blinked... It finally happened–I could sort of human again and in being slapped out of my slight mental breakdown, I became largely aware of my slack jaw and the heavy breathing through what was now the Sahara Desert of my orifice and quickly closed it. Looking down, I busied myself pulling my panties to the side to place him where I knew he wanted to be. He was male, after all... Besides, I had wanted him since seeing his pictures appear on my cell phone. I just wasn't entirely sure how.

And he made me feel things...

Things that were good and scary all at the same time. The stuff stirred in the void, and my god got blotted out and disappeared altogether. In truth to myself, the scariest of all was when he was kind to me, when he saw me and refused to ugly me up.

I needed him to tarnish me, wound me...

Pick and pull me apart and leave me in tatters on the floor amongst the clothes that all of the ones before him had ripped from my flesh. I needed him to stop being all light and sex in the same body because it hurt my feelings and confused the fuck out of me. I felt things and I needed to not. So, I tried to plug him into me to tune out the loud of my heart and mind. But he was not having it. This bull wanted his careful run of my places; his say, his terms, his controlled chaotic way... and I allowed it. He rolled me over onto my back and pulled my thighs up around his hips. There, he had me pinned under his solid frame and took his time to look directly into my eyes.

"May I?" he whispered to me on the floor of that hotel room.

I had no words for the beauty of that moment, so I just nodded my permission, Yes.

25

Chapter 25

Tenderly, he ran his right hand down my body until he reached my panties. Trailing his thick fingers over the curves of my pussy, Garrett slipped a finger beneath. I took in a breath and arched my back. My skin crawled in the way a kitten's fur bunches and tightens when her master runs his fingers through her silky coat. It gave me tingles in all the right ways and in all the right places. My back relaxed and sank into the carpet. I, a melted puddle of sex, lust, and all things provocatively glorious, swiveled my hips up and down greedily, forcing Garrett's fingers deeper into me. Instead of giving me my way, he pulled his hand from my panties and tugged at the thin straps on my hips. Lifting my ass so he could free me of them, he slid them over my thighs and tossed them into the darkness.

I felt the air from the AC rush between my thighs. I clamped my knees shut playfully. The expression on Garrett's face turned quickly to concern. He placed a warm palm on my knee.

"What's the secret password?" I teased, biting my bottom lip.

A deviant smile formed at the corner of his mouth and splashed across his face. There... That one... That smile is the smile that made me smile. It was as infectious as a baby's laughter. You couldn't help but not return it; at least, I couldn't...

His eyes softened, and he kissed my knee cap. I felt it in my vagina. He could tell, so he kissed the side of my knee and paused, watching me shift. My lip slipped from between the grip of my teeth and my mouth hung open, allowing shuddering breaths to escape. Garrett slid his hands down the side of my thighs. My knees began to part of their own accord. I attempted to push them together again to no avail. He had slipped his fingers inside of me from beneath my raised legs.

"Pretty please?" he whispered into my pussy, lowering himself to feast.

His hot breath made me pulse and grind toward his readied mouth.

One lick and one lick only; I moaned and grabbed two handfuls of my own hair.

"Fuck..." I whined needily.

Grabbing my hips to hold me in place, Garrett dove in, and my entire body pulsed with need and pleasure. Soft and firm at all the right times and places. Each flick of his tongue felt like the Fourth of July. Explosions everywhere; and I was a hot fucking mess of a girl with no self-control. I liked losing it...it being my control, my willpower. I like succumbing to my desires and submitting...I loved submitting to...

My god.

The pleasure...

He did that thing with his...

And I- I was delirious, dizzy, my head was spinning. I couldn't tell if it was from the booze or his fucking mouth, but Jesus H. Christ it was magnificent. Garrett's hands gripped my thighs, holding them to the floor. I was opened to him in my entirety. I allowed him to take me to those dizzying floaty places that I adored so much. My spirit did pirouettes inside my bones. My god wasn't the only one capable of making my body sing. There were others and here this man lay; fixed between my legs, worshipping my sacred space and treating as it no less than such-

Sacred...

Hollowed is the ground upon which her body lies; surrendered to the creative powers that be. Sacred is her surrender. Blessed Be-

Sonnet like prayers flitted through my mind. With his tongue alone, he placed me in a space that can be best described as pure poetry. Just when I began to envision myself chiseling out yet another headstone for my second murder, he kissed my pussy. He fucking kissed my pussy. No–this man would not do away with me–this man, he would be my undoing. He wasn't a murderer like my god. He was a Son of the Creative powers that be… He came to undo the damage. He came to rub oil on my bruises; not to poke them and masturbate to my winces. No grave robber was this bull. He came not to rampage in my tiny shop of treasures. He came to lovingly wrap my knick knacks in bubble wrap.

Apon the acknowledgement of this information dropped into my spirit, I grabbed the back of his head and shoved his mouth into me and held him there until my body writhed and twisted like a snake that had just lost its fucking mind. And he stayed; long past the time in which I thought I needed him to. I pushed his forehead when I had had enough, and he obliged my palm by backing away and sitting upright. Garrett wiped his mouth and grabbed my ankles.

I flipped over, my body shuddering from adrenaline and chilled from the air due to lying so still. I pulled myself to kneeling as he slid in behind me, sliding my hair over one shoulder, exposing my neck. I looked over my shoulder and reached around, pulling his neck toward me for a kiss. Kiss me, he did. His hand found its way into my hair, slightly tugging my head, holding it in place. I wasn't planning on going anywhere. I allowed it.

Kat's moans from the other room were accompanied by the loud *clap clapping* of Lucas' hips and bits striking her supple tan-lined ass. I took a moment to feel possessively proud, I silently cheered him on and re-centered myself, so I could be fully present with Garrett. Knowing that my god was in his bliss, I proceeded forward, allowing myself the full experience of pleasure with this new species of man. Letting go of my hair, Garrett's hands explored my body and his mouth ravaged my neck and shoulders. Soft moans floated from my slightly parted lips. I found myself slipping in and out of reality, my head bobbing around limply. His touch and tongue were obscure peony covered gates to other dimensions. And when he pushed himself into me, I was blooming in the bent beam of that hotel bathroom light.

It wasn't the furious frenzied groping grapple that I was used to. When he reached my depths, we took in a sharp breath simultaneously. My petals stretched wide, opening themselves to their capacity and then begged of themselves to stretch a bit more.

Blooming…

And blooming…

And blooming…

My hands shook, my body seized, thighs now locked around his hips. I squeezed him, holding him in place. Garrett obliged and leaned down to breathe me in. He scooped my head into the palm of his hand and wove his fingers into my hair. We clung desperately to one another, panting as I quaked and rumbled. My head lobbed about in his grip. I was beginning the departure process from my body. My spirit had had enough of being confined and needed to purge herself, so she might be able to stretch her limbs into the universe. There wasn't enough room inside me for the two of them to occupy the same space at the same time. He turned me over, bent me over the cushions of the couch, his cock filled me and out she went, right out of my mouth she climbed. And all went silent.

It felt so good I wanted to cry, wail, sob… I howled instead. It was the closest I could come to releasing a combination of the three. I attempted to compose myself and stabilize; Garrett pushed my head and shoulders back down into the couch. I allowed it. My will and body had been weakened from orgasming over and over anyhow. Why fight? His moans had softened. He had let go, this bull was in his floaty space.

I slung my hair over my shoulder and peeked behind me. Garrett's head was back, eyes closed, mouth slightly open…

'It's my turn,' Aurelia sauntered in, switched all the lights off, took me by the vagina, and that's all she wrote. I lifted myself from the cushions, emboldened by the stunning nature of his 'letting go.' I swung my hips and ass up and down his cock, fucking him like my life depended on it. My ass slammed into his hips viciously. His head lowered, our eyes met, and the darkness encompassed him too. I saw when it happened. His face contorted into a painfully-pleasurable, desperate for a soul-deep fuck wince. His breath caught in his throat and his jaw tightened when his hands clutched my hips. I bit my bottom lip and stared directly into his gorgeous darkening eyes as I maneuvered his shaft in and out of me.

"Does that feel good? You like it when I fuck you like this, don't you, baby? Mmmm..." I purred.

When Aurelia Sol arrives, she comes in like a lioness—starving for blood, and sweat, and tears, and phenomenal fucking-orgasms...

And she isn't leaving until she has had her fill and is absolutely sated.

Garrett replied tenderly, "Yes, baby. It feels so good."

I felt myself soften and Aurelia recoiled, hand over her gaping mouth. His voice snatched me back into myself. His voice, hoarse, breathless-calling me baby. It made my heart sigh and turn flips. It calmed my mind and made me gentle. It ripped the holy-fucking-terror that sought to eviscerate, and conquer, and devour from my stomach and poured this alkalizing substance all over her.

"I want to fuck you on the couch," I said to him.

So, we moved to the couch and I slid atop him. I placed him inside of me, wrapped my arms around his neck tightly and kissed him passionately. We rocked together, I howled and whimpered, and held on for dear life, and mercy, and fell apart in his arms—shattered... In a million orbiting pieces inside, I was the most tender eye of the storm and he leaned me backward, holding me securely to him. I let myself fall... Into the safety net of his strong arms, into the gentle of my wild, but more importantly, into the most authentic part of me I had ever experienced in my existence up to that moment.

He pulled my hips back and forth into him, holding me in place, controlling his and my pleasure, using my body to pleasure himself just the way he needed. I let him… I was on the verge of cumming again for the umpteenth time, when I felt Garrett take in a deep breath and hold it. His cock hardened and ached for release inside of me. I squeezed him in a death grip with my pussy. "I-I'm," he stumbled.

"Yes-Yes!"

Moaning and orgasming, I wrapped him up in the cocoon of my arms and quivering legs. As my quaking lessened, I slowed my strokes down and ground my hips into him. Garrett wrapped his arms around my waist, holding me still. I trailed my lips over his, breathing in his bated shuddering breaths, and he breathed in mine. He poured into the condom. I felt him throbbing inside and felt a small sadness that I wasn't able to feel his cum flood into my pussy and seep out of me.

I kissed him and slid off, spent and very sated. We sat beside one another panting.

"Wow…" Garrett allowed his head to lob toward me.

I looked at the ceiling and laughed, "Wow, is an understatement."

I kissed his lips. And we sat there, cooling off, listening to Kat and Lucas' sex sounds.

The slap slapping ceased suddenly, a grunt drifted from the next room, and all went quiet. The bathroom door closed a moment later, leaving us encased in darkness. Garrett's fingers found my pinkie. He wrapped them around mine and I froze, and then melted. I curled my fingers around his. My heart beat out of my chest.

The bathroom door swung open, shining a fluorescent beam on our naked bodies, holding pinkies. Kat stood in the archway between the two rooms. Garrett and I snatched our parts apart and busied ourselves, gathering our clothes and checking in with our respective partners. We said our goodbyes, exchanged pleasantries and promises to do this again sometime very soon. I kept my eyes lowered until following Lucas out the hotel room door. I stole a glance backward at Garrett, whose eyes had been on me the entire time. I smiled at him with my eyes and closed the door.

26

Chapter 26

Lucas and I were both pretty wore out. By the time his diesel rumbled into my neighborhood, I was on autopilot; just staying conscious enough to know when my stop was. The struggle was real, but I managed to gather my bag, give Lucas a peck, and a weak smile before exiting. I didn't bother watching him drive away. One second, I was getting out of his truck, the next, I was collapsing into my bed, and sinking into a deep and very peaceful sleep.

The birds woke me in the morning. I lazily swiped around for my cell. Locating it, I held it in front of my adjusting vision. No messages, no missed calls. The time was 11:32 am. I was due at work in five and a half hours. Pulling the covers back over my head, I drifted off again for another two hours. I awoke to terrible dry mouth and my shirt was twisted around my body. My jeans were twisted around my waist and my undies were hella wedged into my ass. So, I got up and adjusted myself to the best of my 'hung-over' ability. One of my pockets had begun to creep out of my jeans so I shoved my hand into it, tucking the lining back where it belonged.

My fingers tangled in a piece of paper and I tugged it free. *I don't remember putting anything in my pocket. But-I mean...I was pretty drunk, so...* I mulled this tiny folded square over internally before opening it to find a phone number had been scribbled onto it and signed, -Garrett

I realized I was holding my breath when my heart and lungs began to heave themselves against my sternum, begging me to supply them with their much needed life force. I exhaled and took in another. Exhaled and took in another…slowly. I couldn't believe what I was seeing.

"When did he…"

I thought back to moments when Garrett would have had the opportunity to write his number down and place it covertly into my jeans. *That sneaky but brilliant asshole*, I thought. Amused and turned on by his ambition and creativity, I smiled all the way to the coffee pot and lingered there, breathing in the steam and deliciousness. Nothing like a good cup of dark roast to clear the fog.

I downed two cups of coffee, lost in the play by play of last night. I logged on to Facebook and posted a nondescript #AboutLastNight fire emoji, fire emoji, fire emoji. Shoving my phone in my pocket, I floated to the sink, placing my coffee cup in it, floated to the bathroom, showered and dressed for the day, flopped down on my bed… and fell asleep until time to leave for work. On my way out the door, I grabbed a bottle of water and chugged it down, along with three ibuprofens. Off I went, smile on my face and a newer, sexier sway in my hips. Lucas didn't show that evening. I texted him a couple of times and no response. It made me a little sad and pouty inside. But I sucked it up and finished my shift.

Two days had passed and no Lucas. *Radio Silence*! I began to worry that he might have noticed the chemistry between Garrett and me. So, I called.

He picked up on the third ring, "Sure Clean-This is Lucas."

My brain froze; I suppose that I was half expecting him to not answer. "Uh-H-Hi, it's… Um-Amber."

I stumbled. I had to think of what my own name was. *Stupid, what is wrong with you?* I mentally berated myself.

"Well, hey there!" His voice warmed, and I relaxed.

"Hey, you," I smiled into the phone, relaxing some. "I sent you some texts, have you been getting them?"

"I'm sorry, darlin'…I've been busy as shit. Deer Creek Apartment complex caught fire and some pipes burst in other units, my guys and I have been working around the clock to get them cleaned up before mold and mildew and a host of other damage sets in."

I nodded, relieved he wasn't intentionally avoiding me.

"Oh, wow! That sounds like a ton of work. Well, I was just checking in to see when we might be able to go out again. I've been thinking about you."

Silence fell over the conversation. It just dead-ended. It was a punch to the gut. I realized I was coming across as being needed and invested emotionally.

Panicking, I added, "I've been thinking the past few days about how much fun we had with Garrett and Kat. It was really hot, and it turns me on very much, so I was thinking…," turning on my sexy voice, "that I need your cock deep inside of me very soon, terribly so."

Biting my lip, I smiled into the phone and hugged it between my shoulder and ear while tracing and teasing my pussy through my jeans with my fingertips.

"Do you now?" he replied, his voice deepening.

"Mmhmm," I purred into the phone. "I'm playing with my pussy right now thinking of you." I exhaled a shuddering breath loud enough for him to hear it. "I'm imagining your tongue, sliding over it. Flicking at my clit and then maybe sucking on it. Mm-I'm so fucking wet right now, I can feel it through my jeans, Lucas." I moaned softly. "I'm unzipping and unbuttoning my pants now."

In the silence, I heard his breathing quicken. I had his full attention and was reveling in it. "You're going to make it impossible for me to get out of this truck, you know that?"

I tossed my head back and laughed. "That's the plan," I retorted playfully.

"You're feeling very naughty today, huh?"

"Will you have me…tonight? Please?" I begged with my best pouty voice.

"I make no guarantees, but I'll be in touch tonight if I am able to break away from my crew for a bit," he replied.

I sighed audibly to let him know of my disdain.

"I'll do my best!" Lucas reassured me.

"Fine...," I replied, once again pouting and then smiling.

"All right darlin', have a great day. I hope to see you later on."

He ended the call before I could get "Me too," out.

I stared at my cell phone, frowning and empty, horny as fuck, and feeling irritated. I wanted what I wanted, when I wanted it. Sighing a couple of times to calm myself, I looked around my room and decided to call Garrett. He picked up on the first ring.

"This is Garrett."

I smiled from the inside out and my organs did somersaults.

"It's Amber."

He laughed, "You found it. I'm so glad."

I laughed myself, "I did. Very clever, you are."

We enjoyed a giggle together.

"How are you?" he inquired.

"I'm-good. Really good," I replied.

"You sure? It sounds like something is bothering you."

He was good, very observant.

"I-I'm fine. I...," I stammered.

"You don't have to tell me if you don't want to. I understand. You barely know me," he replied.

"Thank you. That is very kind of you. It's just some stuff with Lucas. I-I just really wanted to see him tonight and he is very busy, so I probably won't hear from him and I could really use a good fucking," I confessed boldly.

Silence... When Garrett finally found his voice again, he cleared his throat and laughed saying, "Wow! I would love to help you out with that, if I could."

I laughed seductively into the phone, "Maybe we should make that happen?"

It was more of a question than a statement.

"Oh my god, you don't know how much I'd love to fuck you again," he moaned.

I took a deep breath in, in a pathetic attempt to stop my clit from thudding against the seam of my tight jeans.

"I think I have a pretty good idea...," I said softly.

We sat in silence together, both of us aching for the other's heaving body upon the other.

"So, uh, I'd really like to talk to you about our time together, if you don't mind?"

Breaking the tension somewhat. My spirit did pirouettes in my bones.

"I-I'd really like that. A lot...," I gushed.

"Great, if you don't mind holding for a moment; I need a bit of privacy. I am going to step outside, there are some things about this that I can't speak on in front of Kat."

Garrett shuffled around, and I heard the door swing closed behind him. I heard him walk down the steps, and onto the lawn.

"Okay, are you able to talk freely?" he inquired.

"Yes, absolutely. I'm just in my room; we can talk about whatever you want," I replied, now very curious.

"Phhhh-" He exhaled loudly.

I grew concerned.

"What's wrong? Are you okay?"

"Yes, baby, yes, I am okay. Well, sort of. I don't know. I'm just-I just...Amber, I have never experienced anything like what I experienced with you the other night. My mind is blown. I haven't been able to stop thinking about it. I haven't been able to-" he paused.

I waited for him to finish his sentence.

"Haven't been able to what, Garrett?" I inquired.

"Amber, I can't stop thinking about you, how you smell, your skin is like silk, your beautiful eyes, that mouth... God-I don't know what I am doing. Is this crazy?" He rambled on.

131

My heart hammered in my chest, my head felt swimmy and delirious, my pussy salivated and caved in on itself, and my spirit–she whispered, *Give him your truth and honesty; it is required of you with this one. He needs your truth, he needs your honesty.* So, I gave it to him as hard as I could.

"I knew before I met you that I needed to know you. Lucas sent me photos of you and Kat. I was drawn to you immediately for reasons that are still unbeknownst to me. I just-I... As crazy as it may sound," I laughed and continued, "I trust the unfolding, I trust the process and time will reveal to us the answer to our *Why's* and *How's.*"

"You are wise beyond your years, young lady," Garrett declared.

I squealed inside at his words, *Young Lady... He is beyond dreamy, this one. I am in so much trouble.* I smiled inside, ear to ear and it stretched onto my face.

"Thank you," I began to blush.

"I am so relieved to hear that it isn't just me feeling this way," he said.

"It is definitely not just you. It is a bit scary and very thrilling all at the same time. Because, you know, Lucas and everything," I said quietly, feeling sort of guilty.

"Yeah-" Garrett replied. "So, if you don't mind me asking, what is the story with you and Lucas? What are you two to each other? I know he had said you two were just swing partners?" he continued.

Rolling my eyes, I responded, irritated, "I don't know what we are, honestly. I-"

Garrett cut me off, "You love him, don't you?"

I frowned and grew silent.

"I can tell you do, Amber. Does he not... You know, feel the same or something?" he pressed gently.

"Ultimately, WE are nothing. He told me not to fall in love with him. He is married. His wife doesn't know, I am guessing. He didn't tell me he was married until after we had slept together; so that was awesome," I spat out resentfully.

"But then there lies the fact that he-he makes my body feel incredible.

He is handsome, intelligent, and he brings out aspects of me that I didn't even know existed. Not to mention the fact that all of these things combined make him so goddamned sexy to me. I-he is like a drug; he is my drug. And I-I don't want to, and I am not supposed to but...I..." I stammered, becoming upset.

"But you love him. Baby, you can't help how you feel. Don't beat yourself up over it."

My heart shattered. Tears welled in my eyes. We sat in silence for as long as I needed.

"You deserve better than that, Amber. Do you know that?" Garrett inquired softly.

Blinking, the tears streamed down my cheeks. I swallowed hard.

"I'm trying not to." My voice quivered.

"Are you crying? No... No, no, no, honey. Don't cry. Look, we don't have to talk about him anymore. Let's change the subject, okay?"

I wiped the tears from my face and garbled out a, "Yeah."

"If it makes you feel less alone, for what it's worth, Kat and I haven't been great in a long time. Our relationship is pretty much at the end of the road," Garrett confessed.

"I'm sorry," I replied sympathetically.

"I'm not. I have had enough of her shit. We got into the lifestyle to strengthen our relationship and because we both had an interest in it. At first, it was great, our sex life was amazing, and then it all kind of took a dive when she became less and less interested in being intimate with me when it was time for just us. She does nothing but complain and spew negativity anymore. It stresses me out; I feel alone even when we are together. Quite frankly, that is the worst version of lonely a person could encounter, in my opinion. You know, feeling alone with your partner lying right next to you." He purged himself and then apologized for it immediately afterward.

My heart ached for him. "Wow, Garrett, I-I'm so sorry you are going through that. That is truly awful, and yes, being lonely with your someone special right there is the cruelest form of torture. I experienced that in my marriage. I'm divorced now, but I know how you feel. I can relate."

I sent healing energies quietly through the phone to him.

"Wait, you have been married before? How old are you again?" he inquired.

"I am twenty-one years old," I responded.

He laughed a hearty laugh and sighed exasperatedly.

"What?" I inquired, amused.

"You're just a baby." He laughed again.

"Young, yes… But you were singing a vastly different tune a few nights ago, sweetheart. You didn't seem to mind my age then," I retorted sassily.

"Oh, ho ho hooo! You went there, huh?" Garrett teased.

I shrugged and replied, "It's true, though."

Smiling into the phone, we sat in silence, a stand-off…

"You are correct, baby. And you most definitely do not strike me as a typical twenty-one-year-old. For some reason, I thought you were a little older. I'm not complaining, don't get me wrong- but you just carry yourself with so much grace and poise."

He melted the playful icy show down and my heart all in the same moment.

We both win…

I liked this dynamic. It felt like…like I would imagine coming home should feel; all warm and toasty, tingles and buzzes that bounce around in the pit of your stomach and fluttering in your heart that turns to a *lub lubbing* when the ones you love remind you to remember who you are. He reminds me of who I am to become, the soul I was born into this world with but due to the process, I became more of them and less of me. It resulted in The Humpty Dumpty Effect that was my life. I was perpetually falling off the whatever I was on, shattering; and all of the king's horsemen and all of the king's men couldn't put me back together again.

This exchange is the kind where both people are equally involved in the 'give and take' of pleasure and pain. The responsibility to keep one another's temples holy and sacred, to keep the story as pure and un-retouched as possible so as to never lose sight of the honest to goodness truth of it all, the suffering of it all, the exquisiteness of it all. He is the rare breed of humanity that would take that responsibility as serious as a heart attack; I sensed that he would take a woman's history and spin it into the finest gold, and then… and then, he would braid the strands into her hair and tell her that she adds to the golds value and not the other way around… Never the other way around; because, he knows some things, because he has seen some things, and felt some things. His eyes and the way his energy made my spirit as calm as she was restless at any given moment…

I just knew things about him in the same ways that he just knew things about me. As for me and my house, we had decided from the moment our eyes locked, to take on one another's truths and sometimes even the hurts, spin them into reason and remind one another to be kind not just to others, but most of all, to ourselves… In this exchange, however brief it might be or become, I felt a profound sense of gratitude, the utmost respect, and an ever-deepening affection.

27

Chapter 27

We smiled until our cheeks hurt, lost in meandering conversation from one topic to the next, spilling our guts, and laying our souls bare before one another until the only thing left of us was a simultaneous sigh.

"I know..." I said sadly.

"Yeah, we should go," Garrett agreed hesitantly.

But we kept our phones pressed tightly to our ears, not really wanting to hang up.

"If I asked you to meet with me alone, would you?" he inquired.

My heart skipped a beat. His question hung in the air like mist floating through filtered sun beams on a cool spring morning. A rush of adrenaline surged through my body as my mind ran through the best and worst case scenarios, hitting replay on the extremely naughty ones. I felt the euphoria uncurl and stretch inside of me; it could be best described as the moment when Cinderella's fairy Godmother *bippity boppity booped* her from basic bitch status to queen bitch. A little makeup, a killer outfit, and bomb ass stilettos can go a long way for a girl. You pair those things with the promise of fuckery and poof–sparkles and glitter, and warm fucky feelings everywhere...

"Absolutely, I'd meet you alone," I replied as if Garrett should have known this would be my answer.

My pussy thundered and roared in anticipation of the firming up of the details of our rendezvous. He sighed and laughed. I imagined that he was rubbing his forehead in that moment.

"What?" I asked, grinning devilishly.

"I feel like a teenager."

We both snickered.

"Meet me tonight," I said into the pause.

I waited, heart pounding, vagina shrieking, for his response.

"Kat will be leaving today for a couple days, if you'd like to come over to my place," he offered.

"8 pm?" I replied.

"That is perfect, actually. She heads out around 5 pm."

I nodded, as if he could see me through the phone. Tucking my hair behind my ear, I bit my lip to try and contain my excitement.

"Text me your address, and I will be there."

"I will," Garrett replied softly.

"Okay," I said, equally as soft.

"Okay," he echoed back.

We hung on the phone for another thirty seconds in silence.

"See you soon," I whispered.

"Bye, baby," Garret whispered back.

"Bye...," I whispered, and ended the call.

My phone buzzed as I held it to my chest, smiling like an idiot. It was Garrett's address. This was real... I was going to meet him by myself tonight, just he and I, me and him. *Holy fuck*, I squealed inside, *I am actually going to go through with this.* It occurred to me, for a split second, to let Lucas know what I was going to be doing. And then, I felt a tinge of resentment and decided that this was going to be between Garrett and myself, it was a me thing. He shouldn't be angry with me; after all, he had said that we were "only swing partners."

I grumbled curses under my breath, growing more irritated at the playback of that evening. And then, I felt guilty. I felt guilty because he had told me not to fall in love with him. He had warned me that he wasn't looking for commitment, that he was married... That was a doozy, but I justified my behavior in regard to that one. My heart clawing at Lucas to love it back, constantly scratch scratching at his threshold, only to have the door opened enough to see who it was and then slammed in my face when he realized it was me…

Again.

It was me.

"It's me, isn't it?"

I began spinning, doubting myself. I had never deeply contemplated my worth; I had always assumed that no one gave a fuck about whether I existed or not. So, when someone said they loved me and they proved it by being kind for a few moments, I was always grateful, adoring, but secretly frightened and bewildered, because where I come from, you get your ass handed to you for any or no reason at all and then left with threats of more physical harm if you don't "shut that crying up." Where I come from, the very ones that stand so close to you that their spit lands on your lips while they scream in your face about how they wish they had never adopted you–those people, they are also the same people that threatened to kick anyone's asses that picked on you about your freckles.

So, it was safe to say I was little confused by the whole concept of love, and it was an even larger chance that I had the wrong interpretation of when it was safe to love, and when it was indeed not…safe.

Perhaps, love, as a creature, was entirely perplexing for me, all across the board. So, I found solace in bodies… Bodies that groped me and gripped me tightly to them, hung onto me for dear life, bodies whose mouths pressed against my skin, their raspy voices heaving words of worship and praise into my ears. Bodies that pushed me away and then quickly pulled me back in; in those bodies, I found purpose and warmth. They needed me. And I needed to be needed, wanted, even if it meant I was nothing more than one exceptional orgasm. In that moment–I was desperately wanted. I was used to being thrown away; that, I could handle. I reveled in my god's desire for me, his lust was intoxicating and all it took was one look from Lucas, and my humanity fucked off. He needed me, and I needed him, and that was going to have to be enough.

I was getting the feeling that the dynamic between Lucas and I fell along the spectrum of me being the young, fun, rowdy, reckless girl from the wrong side of the tracks–I had issues in all the right places and I fucked like I had just come home from the war. I didn't know how to nor did I care to hide my dirty like all of the socialites he was used to in his world; no... Lucas didn't love 'girls like me.' He didn't marry girls like me.

He fucked girls like me...

And that was going to have to be enough. I was going to have to repeat that to myself until I became okay with it, that was going to have to be enough. We would cease to be if I pushed for more and I knew it.

Whatever Lucas and I were–this limbo 'thingy mah'jig'...was I angry about it? On the surface, it appeared so, it appeared more like annoyance, to be honest; while inside, the recesses screamed, "wounded again, get me away from myself, someone, please." But it was so much easier to show anger and bitterness, throw "a temper tantrum," "be bratty," and "act out," than it was to risk exposing my true pain to Lucas and have him leave my life. I sucked it up, got my ass on my shoulders about it, and stepped on the gas...to Garrett's house I went. The reward outweighed the risk this time; sorry statistics, not sorry.

It was 7:45 PM when I arrived; showtime. Garrett greeted me with a soul-warming hug that lasted so long that when he took his arms from around me, I felt cold. I hadn't realized I was chilled until then. I noted it as oddly romantic and we moved into his house. He had a tan sectional couch, palmetto tree prints framed in golds and silvered bronze metals. I noted a wicker chair with intricate braiding along the back rest in the corner. A flash of my pale white legs draped over the dramatically curled arms of the chair blazed its way into my line of vision. I stood there, enraptured by the daydream of his tongue gliding across my aching pussy. He asked me if I was okay, if I wanted something to drink. I snapped back to attention and tucked my hair behind my ear, smiling as if I had not been busted.

"I am. Yes… Tequila. Margarita?" I sputtered.

Garrett squinted and furrowed his eyebrows, returning my smile. "You sure you're okay?"

I let out an audible 'phhbbtt.' His eyebrows shot up and his smile turned sideways. I pushed him playfully.

"What were you thinking just then?" Garrett inquired.

According to the butterflies in my stomach, he already knew; he just wanted to hear me say it, and maybe give details. We stared into one another's eyes. The smiles fading slowly into the thundering in our chests. I ran my fingers down his abdomen and touched his belt.

Stepping in closer to him, I cooed seductively into his jaw line, "Maybe…I should just whisper it into your ear."

He took in a sharp breath, his jaw tensed, and I could feel movement in the front of his jeans as I pressed my body into his and swayed with one arm around the back of his neck. A soft moan pushed past his lips as he nuzzled them against my ear. I brought his face to mine, lingered—breathing in his warm exhale, just before allowing our lips to meet, and kissed him deeply.

Pulling away from his mouth, I pushed his head to the side and held it there, whispering into his ear, "I was daydreaming about how amazing it would feel to sit in your wicker chair, legs over the arms, and have your tongue sliding over my pussy until I came."

He bit his lip and laughed. That laugh though… It held so much promise. So, I continued to press buttons, trying to find which one sent him over the edge, to the point of no takebacks. I brushed his cock with my fingers and palm while staring into his eyes. Maintaining eye contact with him, I saw the wince. It was subtle, but I caught it. I had seen it in the hotel room, while I fucked him staring directly into his eyes. My touch was his torch.

It was my touch, my energy, that drove him to the precipice, to that place that hurt so fucking good. So, I touched him again… This time, grabbing a handful of him and stroking it through his jeans. His head tilted backward, eyes closed, mouth slightly open, right hand tangled into the hair at the nape of my neck, Garrett moved suddenly and with a quickness I had never seen. One second, I was rubbing his cock, dead set on making him cum in his pants, the next second, I was against the wall adjacent to us, hands, palm down, at my sides, my pants around my ankles, shirt pushed up to my rib cage.

"Is this what you wanted, young lady? My tongue in that gorgeous pussy?"

His fingers wove their way into my folds. My legs weakened, head still spinning from literally being spun around and slammed into a wall, I nodded my approval.

"You're so fucking wet already," Garrett said, shocked.

"I-I've been thinking about you a lot since… and then our–fuck-kkkkk!"

My hands flew up and into my hair as his mouth found my clit. I felt like I was melting. I began sliding down the wall. Garrett caught me and held me against it and himself. Bent over and, holding onto the wall, all at the same time, my hips swiveled on his jaw autonomously.

"Fuck… Fuck… Fuck. It feels so fucking good," I whined and ground my hips into his face harder.

"Yes," Garrett mumbled, his mouth full of me. "Mmm, you taste so good." He moaned into my folds.

I pressed my hand into the back of his head, holding it in place, orgasming over and over. This magical place, it was the gateway to the portal of transcendence, a place where divinity pervaded all of my nature and all of my humanity.

I rode the waves of pleasure into shore. As the pangs and throbbing subsided, I realized that my legs had turned to quivering jelly. So, I stood unsteadily, leaning against the wall for support. Reality, still hazy but coming more and more into focus, I became aware of my pants and underwear that were now only clinging to one ankle, in a wad, on the floor. Garrett stood, wiping his mouth clean of me on his forearm. He shot me a hungry look paired with a devious sideways smile. Still catching my breath, I smiled weakly at him and smeared my forearm across my lips, biting down on it for a few seconds. My pussy throbbed again from the feeling of my own flesh gripped between my teeth. It hurt so fucking good.

I wanted his cum desperately. I wanted to feel him explode inside of me, but I knew better at the moment, while my head was still somewhat clear. So, I dropped to my knees and returned the favor until he pushed firmly into my mouth moaning, cock throbbing and feverish.

"God, baby. Yes. Yes- Mm. Those lips... god, your mouth is heaven."

I swallowed him down and stood, woozy from the adrenaline. My pussy was dripping down my thighs.

I turned my ass to him as he stepped closer. Pulling my hair over my shoulder, I exposed my neck and peeked back at him. Garrett's strong hands cupped my ass, giving it an admiring bounce and playful smack.

"Tell me what you want, baby."

He nuzzled the impossibly soft place between my neck and shoulder. My pussy quaked. I pressed my forehead into the wall and smeared it across its surface as his hands roamed my body, grabbing my breasts, my hips, my ass, and sliding his fingers over my wetness.

"I need you inside of me so badly," I said softly.

My desires were purely carnal in this moment. I ached and pined for the moment of penetration. I felt the desire so deeply that I swore I could feel it in my teeth. It was a pushing, pulling, stretching.

Finally, my body screamed like a banshee. Garrett pushed into me, my hips bucked wildly in response. I needed to be fucked. This was not the time nor the moment in which to be sweet to me.

"Fuck me," I demanded.

He had been trying to hold me still, so he could slowly slide in and out of me, savoring the sensations. *There will be time for the sweet stuff, my bull. For now, I need to be blown apart, I need to be exorcised. Deliver me, please,* my body begged of him. He obliged my body's language and pushed my head into the wall, pulled my hips and ass outward toward him for ease of access, gripped a handful of my hair, and slammed into me. I bellowed a cry so loud it echoed through his house.

He held himself inside of me and growled, "Is this what you need, baby?"

Nodding my head in approval, I squeezed my eyes shut, waiting, bracing, preparing. *Here we go,* I thought. And, we went... For an hour, Garrett pushed me, pulled me, pinned me, and ultimately, over the cliff we went together.

Over a cliff...

The adventure of the headfirst dive into the abyss is rather delightful when a shared experience. His cock twitched inside of me as he held my hips stationary. I squeezed him tightly, so he could feel my pussy contracting and stayed as still as possible for him. Garrett pulled out and stripped the condom off. He fumbled around as I was coming down from whatever altitude. He had slipped back into his pants and then kissed me on my shoulder blade.

"May I use your restroom?" I asked, using my best manners.

I was absolutely deep in my submissive kitten place, all coo's and purring, a belly full of Daddy's warm milk, a sated pussy.

"Of course! It is down the hallway, second door on the left."

I kissed him passionately and lingered, smiling like an idiot–happy... just happy. He smiled back and gave my ass a playful smack,

"Go get cleaned up, I'll mix some drinks and make your plate. I made baked chicken and vegetables for us."

I bit my lip, kissed him again, and headed to the shower.

28

Chapter 28

Time flew as it always does when two souls are lost in moments, fully engaged, drunk, and falling-falling-falling in…love. Unfortunately, also, as reality has a tendency to shove it's intrusive ass in where it doesn't belong, life and responsibilities rang the doorbell and before I knew it, it was time to leave. We clung to one another beside the car door, in the cool damp of the 3 AM hour.

"Is it wrong for me to feel this way?" Garrett inquired.

He knew instinctively that I knew precisely what 'this way' meant. He knew, because he could read my soul as if he had known me my entire life, and perhaps, all of the lifetimes before.

I felt a tinge of guilt. Here I was, falling for another man that wasn't mine to fall for, feeling guilty because I was, once again, encroaching upon another woman's territory; feeling guilty because I was, once again, secretly giving my love and body to a man that was not whom I had sworn my heart to–even if Lucas didn't want nor deserve it; feeling guilty because I was lying again…

What was wrong with me? My mind spun wildly behind my eyes. My sad eyes looking at him looking at me, searching my face for the answer.

I sighed.

He needed me in this moment, it was crucial that I give him what he needs.

So, I answered, "No. It isn't wrong. The heart wants what it wants, and who are we to deny ourselves happiness that we deserve?"

I lied... We both looked down at our hands interlaced. Silence fell, we both knew it was wrong; neither of us wanted to admit it. But we wanted to give the other what we both needed more than anything else in the universe—a home; a space to be whomever we were and nothing and no one else to anyone, a safe place to stockpile the overflow of love and trust we had to give.

And if we must feed each other lies to keep our hearts full, even if only for a moment, then let our emptied hearts feast. Let us eat and drink of one another and know. We both knew, we knew that the timing was all wrong. We knew that we had just waded into muddy waters and bathed ourselves in it, us two performing a baptism of our grief-one for the other. But there was no making it pure or making it go away when what is done in the dark is done. Muddy or not, we fucked, and the heartbreak was palpable, but not because we regretted our time together, no... A little because there were now secrets we were keeping from Kat, and a little because there were now secrets I was keeping from Lucas.

But mostly, it was because we knew, deep down, that the homes we were molding out of one another, they would never be permanent. We were the fleeting summer season on the coast of South Carolina, in the middle of August's storms; all roaring thunder and heat lightning, seeking, stretching for ground to be absorbed into, and seeking a source when no one was looking. We were parallel lines, running alongside one another. We were so close, but never fully touching.

Woman, thy name is Catharsis. This name, it waltzed in and seated itself in my soul. I kissed his forehead as he leaned in for a kiss.

"I should really get going," I said.

Garrett nodded and stepped back. "If I don't see you again-" he began.

I stopped just before stepping into the car, my back turned to him, I glanced down and to the side, waiting for him to finish.

"I would understand. But... I-" he paused and let out an audible sigh.

I turned to face him. His eyes pleaded with me once again, searching my face for the next right thing to say.

"You will see me again, Garrett."

Relief washed over him and he grabbed my hand.

"Please, kiss me before you go."

I looked at the ground and watched my feet step back toward him, my arms wrapped around his neck and his around my waist, our foreheads touched, and we lingered in this beautiful moment of intimacy, swaying to the frequency of melding energies, and a symphony of crickets, frogs, and Katydids under a sky full of stars. The kiss felt like saying goodbye. His sadness permeated my lips and broke my heart into bits. I pulled away from him and looked into his eyes.

"I promise, you will." I reassured him.

He nodded, and I got into the car.

I didn't look in my rearview mirror on the way out. I couldn't bring myself to. I could feel his heartbeat slowly pounding in the way a heart would as it were dying.

BUMP (long pause) BUMP BUMP.

I wasn't sure how it was possible to be so in tune with another soul and so quickly, but it was happening. We were in the thick of something. My soul was loving this stranger that didn't feel at all like a stranger, and he was loving me back; neither of us really being able to comprehend why just yet. We just knew our bodies needed to remain touching, our energies blending, and we needed to keep talking, even if neither of us had a word to say, we just needed... So, we were taking. We were a lot alike, Garrett and me. Perhaps it was like looking in a mirror and not being able to recognize yourself; seeing something vaguely familiar and not being able to put a finger on why it seems you've experienced this person before.

* * *

I made it home, trudged my emotionally drained ass into bed, and slept like a baby until the birds woke me up singing and chirping away. It was 7 AM, and I needed to begin my day. I got up, downed some water, dressed and did my hair and makeup, headed to the coffee pot and off to work I went.

Garrett and I were silent for a couple of days. Lucas had finally made an appearance, though.

He buzzed my cell, "What are ya doing, darlin'? I feel like I haven't seen you in forever."

Silence…

"Yeah, I've just been working and stuff," I replied, feeling a pang of guilt.

More silence…

"Mmhm," Lucas added. "Are you sure that is all?" he pressed.

My heart skipped a couple of beats. Did he know? *Oh my god, he knows. He knows. Shit,* I began to freak out inside.

"Yes!" I spat back at him, a little too defensive.

Another silent pause ensued. *He's definitely suspicious,* I worried.

"Are you free tonight?" Lucas asked.

"For you, of course!" I replied, trying to sound more upbeat and flirtier.

"You have other options, do you?" he quipped back.

Full panic mode– "What? No! What would make you ask me that?" I squeezed the phone to my ear.

"No reason. I was just teasing you," he replied in a grave tone.

Get yourself together, Amber. If he didn't suspect anything before, he most certainly does now! I scolded myself internally.

"Not funny," I said, putting on my best pouty voice.

"Oh, come on now…," he teased, his tone lightening.

"What did you have in mind, when you asked if I was busy tonight?" I inquired, changing the subject altogether.

"I have a really hot couple in mind, their names are David and Marie, and I have tickets to The Comedy House for us. What do ya say, drinks, some laughs, some friends, and then I want to watch you fuck David's wife on my boat," he stated, very matter-of-factly.

My eyebrows shot up and I sat back in my office chair.

"Wow," I laughed.

Lucas chuckled softly. "What do you say?" he pressed.

"Well, it isn't often that I am at a loss for words, but uh… admittedly, I-I am at the moment. That surprised me. But to answer your question, yes. What time should I be ready?" I replied.

"I'll pick you up around 8 PM, show starts at 9 PM. See your sexy ass soon."

I smiled into the phone, intrigued and slightly turned on.

"See you then," I replied.

We hung up, and I floated through the rest of the day, my thoughts drifting back to Garrett and Kat every so often, wondering if he had told her, how he was feeling, and if I should maybe just send a lifeline text– "thinking of you…" "hope you're okay…" I decided not to, just in case Kat had access to his phone. I didn't want to make matters worse, so I stayed silent.

29

Chapter 29

Carefully coifed, perfectly fragranced, and the lips a deep but bold red, I smiled at my reflection as I checked my teeth while I awaited Lucas' appearance at my side of the truck. The door opened, I tucked my bag under my arm, and took his hand. I adored the times in which he treated me like a princess; opening my doors, pushing my chair in as I sat, his hand possessively Dominant on the small of my back—leading me with a gentle firmness. It is the stuff that my sexiest dreams were made of.

The lights were dim inside the club. Some round tables smattered here and there, and one larger L-shaped table to the right side of the stage; that's where our party was sitting. David was tall with broad shoulders, dark brown hair, light eyes, a dazzling smile, tanned, and muscular but in a sexy dad kind of way. He rose to greet us. Marie saw David rising from his seat and glanced in our direction. She stood, flashing an equally dazzling grin. Grabbing for my hands, she kissed each cheek and pulled back to look me over.

"My god, your pictures don't do you justice."

I flushed and looked down, tucking my hair behind my ear.

"I hope that is a good thing," I said, not wishing to appear egotistical.

I knew I was stunning, but the vibe that I felt said, *Be gracious, for now.* Marie held my hands and smiled at me admiringly.

"Don't be modest. You know you're gorgeous, isn't she, Dave?"

I gently tugged my hands free from Marie and flashed a smile to her husband. Lucas shook David's hand and I stepped forward, giving him a very polite one armed hug. We all sat down and ordered drinks.

"$15.00 for a freaking midori sour? Are you kidding me?" I hissed in Lucas' ear as the server walked away.

"You do not worry about that. You enjoy the show. Later, that ass is mine."

I looked straight forward, biting the inside of my lip and shifted in my seat.

Let the show begin…

Twenty minutes into the comic's set, Marie and Lucas began exchanging fuck me eyes. So, I politely excused myself to the ladies room, freshened up, checked my phone for any missed calls or messages. Nothing from Garrett. I allowed myself a moment of sadness and self-loathing, shoved my cell back into my bag, and upon making it back to our table, I strategically placed myself beside David, kissing Lucas on the way past him and giving him a wink. He grazed my hand and winked back. Marie scooted in closer to him. Hands disappeared under the table, and then there was us… David and I, we sat there like two bumps on a log. Not really any chemistry to speak of. I was disappointed, to say the least, when I realized he wasn't a man of much substance, neither above or below his belt line. *Maybe he was great with his mouth?* I wondered secretly.

Making small talk with him was like pulling teeth. Perhaps, he was just nervous, so I did what anyone in my situation would have done; I placed my lips to his ear lobes and cooed into his ear about how he was going to watch me fuck his wife later. I grabbed his cock, and then planted a luscious, sexy, breathtaking kiss right on his lips. I felt his tongue slip into my mouth a few times, just in light swipes.

There was a dynamic to be respected; and if the pair of them were both submissive, we must restore balance. I poured three more drinks down my throat. By the fifth, I was burning up, in more than one way. My pussy was shrieking, mewling, and scratching at the ever-dampening thin layer of cotton and satin covering it. She wanted out too. While the gentlemen took a bathroom break during intermission, I scooted closer to Marie. A beautiful petite blonde until you follow the lines of her body down to her thighs; there, she thickened out, and it was glorious. My mouth watered, imagining what was beneath those fucking thigh highs that peeked out when she crossed and uncrossed her legs. And it didn't help matters any that the more she drank, the higher her tight little dress went up those thighs.

Between the booze and those curves and nylons wreaking havoc on my senses, my defenses were down, and the graciousness I had begun the evening with, had disappeared.

"Have you ever been with a woman before, Marie?" I inquired, playing with tiny tendrils of her hair.

She smiled broadly, "A couple of times. I find it very erotic. There is just something about a woman's body that turns me on so very much." She gushed.

I zoomed in on her lips, how they pulled themselves apart as she formulated her words, the hints of her pink tongue between her teeth as she spoke, how she licked her full lips before every sip from the little straw in her Malibu Bay Breeze.

"Lucas wants to watch me fuck you. Did you know that?"

I gauged Marie's response time; this was news to her. She touched her collar bone and sipped her drink, and then tucked her hair behind her ear.

Too shy to look directly at me as she said it, she looked straight ahead and replied, "I'm really flexible."

I grinned from ear to ear and squeezed her thigh, "Good to know, because tonight, your feet are going to be firmly planted on the ceiling of his boat, while my face is planted firmly in that gorgeous pussy of yours."

Marie bit her lip and grinned. She shot me an eyebrow wiggle and leaned in close as the men made their way back to the table, "Deal."

I nodded, acknowledging our understanding, and switched seats with her.

"You guys looked like you were in a pretty deep conversation. Anything good?" Lucas inquired.

Nonchalantly, I replied, "I was just telling Marie that her feet were going to be firmly planted on the ceiling of your boat tonight."

He leaned out and looked at me with a deviant gleam in his eyes.

"Is that so?" he retorted, surprised at my boldness.

"Oh, it is so." I patted his leg.

We both smiled at one another knowingly until the show was almost over. We had all had enough, bellies full of booze and burgers, and a never ending supply of lust. We could have powered a major metropolitan area if our drives and energies could be harnessed and converted, I was certain of it. They followed us back to Lucas' slip.

The water looked like black silk against the crescent sliver of moonlight that shone down. A slight warm breeze was blowing in the smell of the ocean. Stars dotted the heavens, like perfect freckles upon the face of perfection. It was the perfect evening. We were drunk, in no pain physically or emotionally, and naked strangers making eyes. Well, Marie and I were naked strangers who had an understanding. I was going to fuck her exceptionally well.

"You might walk over here girl, but you're limping back."

I may or may not have said this out loud and in all seriousness to someone...

Lucas and David were drinking beers and talking fishing and other sorts of small talk. Marie lay on the bed. I stood at the end, admiring her beauty. Touching her foot, she looked down at me, watching intently. I grabbed her big toe and wiggled it back and forth playfully. She giggled for a second, the smile faded from her face. I could tell she was ready for me. So, I slid onto her body, and touched her, caressed her, pulled her into me, and kissed her seductively.

Her body writhed, and she ground her pussy onto my fingers.

"Do you want more?" I breathed into her mouth.

Marie moaned her approval. I sat back on my knees and readied myself to lick her until she came on my face. We began with her legs over my shoulders, nice… and easy. Slow, long strokes of my tongue along each side of her labia, just brushing the sides of her clit. Her thighs quivered every time she felt my hot breath and warm tongue near it.

"Fuck…," Marie whined. "Please, please lick it, Amber. Please… Pleeeeassseeee!"

She grabbed my head, shoving it forcefully into her pussy. I obliged her and stayed put on her little bud. Grabbing her thighs and pulling her ass into me, dinner plate style, her legs shot up into the air, thighs quivering. Her feet, planted firmly and flat against the ceiling of Lucas' boat.

He stood at the end of the bed, my ass in the air, him working his fingers in and out of my hole, slowly at first and then rough and hard; just the way I adored it. I began to moan and fuck his fingers while I tongue fucked Marie. She came hard, squirting down my left cheek, my chin, my neck, and into my cleavage.

Lucas stepped back to allow us time to clean up and recuperate. He and David stepped back out of the cabin. I could hear them laughing and something about "goddamn, we are lucky sons a bitches." Beer bottles clanked in our honor.

"I want you now, I mean, I'd like to try," Marie offered quietly.

I smiled softly. "Yes," I accepted.

"I uh-Would-would you sit on my face?" she inquired so cautiously it made me laugh out loud.

Her face fell.

"No! I mean, yes to sitting on your face but no to me laughing at you. I wasn't laughing at you just then. I swear, the way you asked me to sit on your face was the cutest shit I think I have ever seen. It was endearing," I explained.

She relaxed, and we shared a giggle over it.

"You were amazing, and I don't have a lot of exp−"

I shushed her by kissing her.

"Don't explain yourself to me. You don't have to, I understand."

Marie smiled kindly at me and looked down.

"Hey, don't do that. Don't feel insecure. You are incredibly beautiful and passionate, and open; you are learning and experiencing. Don't feel embarrassed, okay?"

She beamed back at me, "Just wow, Amber. Where did you come from?"

I waved a hand of dismissal and broke the intimacy, "I'm going to fuck your face now, Marie."

I sat on her face mid-sentence.

* * *

Passing by David on my way off the boat, he seemed aloof. He had seemed aloof all night, which unsettled me some. I nodded my head politely as I brushed by him.

"Your wife is lovely," I mentioned, leaning in to him.

He took a swig of his beer and smiled.

"She is, isn't she?" he retorted.

The first ray of sunshine and warmth all night. He might actually have a personality in there–somewhere… I patted his chest. Lucas helped me onto the floating dock and I placed my heels on after getting off the boat this time.

As we were saying our goodbyes, David asked about sleeping arrangements. I froze.

"Wait… what? They're spending the night? With you? On the boat?" I squeaked out.

Here I was, being dismissed so that these people could stay? WHAT? I was livid and slightly confused. Lucas took a swig of his beer.

"Yes, they're staying. They drove in from North Carolina to see us. They will head back tomorrow morning."

I took this in and chewed on it, while staring David down.

Images of hot, sweaty, incredible sex that I wouldn't be a part of or privy to swirled in my mind.

"Why do they have to stay on your boat? Can't they just get a hotel room?" I asked.

Lucas looked annoyed.

"Are you going to have sex with her? I mean, you didn't–don't you think you should have at least mentioned it to me that they were going to be staying with you on the boat?"

He answered none of my questions. He sipped his beer with a stern look on his face. He wouldn't even make eye contact with me.

I knew…

They had already planned this. They wanted me gone, but most of all, Lucas wanted me gone so that he could rejoin his friends on the boat for a fuck-fest that I had just been kicked out of, and promptly at that. The range of feelings I was experiencing all at once had my head spinning. I imagined that I looked like one of those cartoon characters with smoke pouring out of their ears and buggy eyes. Lucas and I stood in silence; me staring at him and then to Marie and David who saw the tension and surprise on my face when I learned of the plans that were made without my knowledge or input, and him staring out over the water, looking at anything but me, stone faced, jaw tightened.

Feelings of regret and fear began rushing in. I went too far. I had–I had gone too far. *He won't want to see me again after shooting my mouth off to him.* My mind raced erratically.

"Hey," I spoke softly as I put my hand on his elbow.

Lucas didn't flinch. Letting my hand drop, I stood behind him, crushed. I just wanted to wrap myself around him, but it felt like he didn't want me anywhere near him. Boldly, I walked toward him and wrapped my arms around his waist tightly and buried my face between his shoulder blades.

We stood quietly for a moment and then he gripped my arms and rubbed my hand softly.

"I'm sorry. I'll go, okay? Call me tomorrow?" I inquired, hopeful.

"I will, darlin'," he replied as he broke my grip and turned to face me.

Lucas wrapped an arm around my neck and pulled my forehead

to his lips. I closed my eyes and lingered. Looking down, not really wanting to leave, he pulled my chin upward. We locked eyes, my heart raced. He gazed tenderly at my face, settling on my lips. Moving in and pulling my face to his, he planted a passionate kiss on my lips.

I melted into my broken heart, a sea of chaos departing.

Churning and burning up inside, I walked away fighting tears back. I was painfully aware of my posture. My shoulders must be raised and my spine straight and strong. Something inside me was terrified of making him uncomfortable with the fact that I was crumbling on the inside, that it was killing me to be the one he chose to send away instead of them, and it mustn't ever show again that I was dying. Not in what I spoke, not in the way I carried myself, and never in my eyes was I ever, under any circumstances, allowed to allow myself freedom of the outward expression of emotions. It upset him; I upset him. And now, there I was, walking that goddamned dock back to my car. It was forever a sentence to disconnect—a sending away, a 'fuck off, honey'. And, I hated it, I hated it, I hated it with all of my heart.

Loved coming, loathed going.

Driving home, I allowed the tears to stream down my cheeks. The feeling of rejection touched my soul deeply. It gnawed at me, shredded me. I flung myself onto my bed at whatever time it was that I had trudged my eviscerated hot mess into the house and cried myself to sleep. The next day came and went with no word from Lucas. My heart knew back on the dock that I wouldn't hear from him. So, with torturous contempt, I waited.

30

Chapter 30

The work days drug on for the first weeks of not hearing from him. I walked around feeling like a caveman dragging his boulder of a heart around by the hair. Garrett had been in touch and proposed the idea that I become a subcontractor cleaning the showrooms for his company for some extra cash. Deciding that busy and extra money was greatly needed in my life at the moment, I took him up on his offer and met with him to discuss the details.

Black dress pants, black silk dress shirt donning red cherries, strappy heels, of course my intoxicating jasmine and orange blossom perfume later, and I headed toward Garrett's office. I texted him to let him know I had pulled in. Walking in, he rose from his desk, beaming. Coming around his desk, Garrett kissed my cheek and seated me.

"Thank you," I responded, sitting and crossing my legs.

We sat across from one another smiling.

"It's really good to see you again," he said.

I nodded politely and smiled sweetly. "It is really good to see you too. Thank you for offering this position," I replied.

He laughed and rubbed his forehead, his cheeks turning slightly red. *I know, Garrett... Trust me, I know. Yes, it is what you think I meant. I am burning up too*, I thought secretly.

"Okay, so let's jump into the details." He curtly changed the subject, clearing his throat.

I shifted into business mode and we hammered out and fine-tuned until we were clear and both on the same page.

"You make it virtually impossible to concentrate, you know that?" Garrett inquired.

"Yeah?" I replied innocently.

He smiled at me, squinting slightly, peering into me, "I think you know you have that power. I think you enjoy making men feel uncomfortable."

We stared at one another.

I shrugged coyly, "Perhaps."

His smile faded, and he grew somber and intense.

"You love it, don't you? You like knowing that my cock is rock hard under my desk, right now."

I bit my bottom lip as my pussy began throbbing.

I nodded, yes.

"There are so many things I'd love to do to you, right now. Mostly, I want to bend you over and fuck you on my desk with the door unlocked so that someone could walk in, at any moment, and catch me fucking you."

I swallowed hard and my heart thundered.

"What would you do if I took you right now?" Garrett inquired.

"I'd let you," I replied quietly.

He stood and walked slowly toward me. Standing behind me, he place his hands on my shoulders, squeezing them. I took in a deep breath to steady my racing heart. He pulled my hair to one side, tossing it over my shoulder, exposing my neck and ear. I tilted my head to give him ease of access, and closed my eyes, taking another deep breath.

"Would you like for me to tell you what you do to me?"

So captured by the moment, my words wouldn't formulate. So, I just nodded my head, yes.

Garrett leaned down, brushing his lips against my ear, sending shivers down my spine. Goosebumps covered my body. I allowed a soft moan to push past my lips. "Mm."

He began running his hands over my neck and collarbone, squeezing ever so lightly here and there. My breaths grew shaky. I could feel the wetness leaking from my pussy. I was going to be soaking wet by the time he was finished with me, I just knew it. I probably already was. I was getting a bit squirmy, until he spoke and gripped my throat.

"What are you doing to me, Amber?" He pressed his mouth to my ear, so I could hear his whispers.

My hips began to sway back and forth in my chair and then my back began. As the waves of pleasure rolled through me, my body bent and bowed to it, honoring it, and begging it back. *More please*, my mind screamed.

"You make me feel things, dangerous things, young lady," Garrett whispered into my ear.

His breath was deliciously hot. Pangs of pleasure shot through me. I wrapped my arm around the back of his neck and rubbed my cheek into his face.

"Are your panties wet, little girl?" he growled.

I moaned and rolled around to standing. We grabbed one another, kissing with feverish abandon. I placed his hand down the front of my pants.

"Fuck," Garrett whispered. "You are so fucking wet. I love how wet you get. I want my tongue in your pussy, baby."

"Mmm," I moaned, a little louder this time. "Please? Yes?" I begged.

Garrett spun me around to face his metal filing cabinet, shoved his hand down my pants again, found my clit, and within minutes, had me crumbling in orgasm. I held onto the corner of the metal frame, knees buckling, Garrett holding me up with one hand and insisting I orgasm completely and entirely with the other.

"Fuck!" I moaned loudly.

His hand went from holding me up to my mouth and clamped my lips shut tightly.

"Shh, not too loud, baby. Unless you want the entire office to know you're getting fucked." He hissed into my ear.

"I don't fucking care, I don't… It feels so good," I cried out.

"Mm, that's my naughty girl," he cooed into my ear and slapped my ass, cupping it and squeezing, pulling me into his throbbing hard cock possessively.

He pulled his fingers free from my pussy, licking them clean.

"You taste so fucking good," he hissed into my ear.

I turned to face him and planted a sexy kiss on his lips. My left hand roamed down his body and onto his cock. Grabbing him through his slacks, I rubbed up and down, writhing my body into his and moaning into his mouth.

"Fuck me, please?" I begged.

"Mm-You are insatiable; as much as I want to, I probably shouldn't. I do have other meetings that will be arriving soon. And I still have to wash up and get this guy to go down." Garrett nodded down toward his member protruding from his pants.

We shared a laugh, straightened ourselves out, said our goodbyes, and I headed back home.

"Soaked," I texted to him once home and undressing for the shower.

Moments later, my phone buzzed. "and delicious," he responded, adding a smiley face with its tongue sticking out.

I laughed out loud, shaking my head, put my phone down, and showered. I needed that reprieve. I was so grateful for the brief moment that I was able to forget that my heart was in pieces.

It felt nice to be wanted. The orgasm wasn't a terrible ending to a superb beginning either.

31

Chapter 31

32 days, 6 hours, and 3 minutes...

That's how long it had been since I have heard from him. He summoned me to his office.

Lucas: My office in 20 minutes. See you then?

Obediently, I went.
Like I had a choice.
Magnets, with poles aligned properly, do not willingly separate; they get pulled apart by outside forces forcing their wills upon them, but it is their innate will to always be attracted to one another and ultimately, their body will crash into the other with feverish abandon. It is need, it is law, the law of attraction; and when thy will be done, all will be made right in their world.
I waltzed in with my nose in the air. He noticed, and I considered that a teensy tiny victory.
"What's wrong?" Lucas inquired.
I sat in the chair on the other side of his desk. I didn't kiss him or attempt to touch him in any way. I looked down and shook my head as I fumbled with my fingers.
"Nothing. I'm fine," I lied.

He stared at me until I looked at him.

"You said you wanted to talk to me. I'm here," I cut straight to the chase, attempting to be stone.

His eyebrows shot up. He straightened papers on his desk then sat back in his chair, crossing his legs, and clasped his hands behind his head.

"You sure nothing is wrong?"

I stared at him, confused. "One minute, you act as if you couldn't care less and the next, you are super concerned about how I am feeling?"

I attempted to sort this concept out in my head.

"I-why?" I blurted out.

Lucas stared at me blankly.

"Why? Where have you been?" I stammered.

Lucas cleared his throat and closed his posture. Uncrossing his legs, placing them together, hands on the desk clasped together, head down, he took a sip of his beer.

"I told you not to fall in love with me, Amber. What in the hell was that, at my boat, when Marie and David were visiting?" he questioned me.

I looked down, my cheeks flushing from embarrassment. I took a moment to collect myself.

"I know you said to not fall in love with you, Lucas. I heard you. I have tried, and I have fought it so hard. I-I am in love with you, and I am so sorry."

Tears streamed down my face. The flood gates had opened and all of the shit I had been holding on to since meeting this enigma of a man was now ugly crying all over his office. Lucas' jaw tensed, he rubbed his forehead and once again, refused to look at me, to see me, bear witness to my pain, to acknowledge it.

And, it fucking hurt like hell to see, once again, but truly, this time, that I would have to endure this alone, that he would offer me no consolation. Reality was a stark, cold slap in the face.

"Goddamn it, Amber," Lucas sighed.

"I'm sorry. I've just been holding this in for a long time. I'll do better, I promise." I began apologizing profusely for my feelings, for causing a scene, for making him uncomfortable, for going against his rules, for being a human being with feelings.

"No," he began. "Come here to me."

Lucas handed me several tissues. I wiped my face and nose. I was so upset that I had begun hyperventilating. Approaching him, I stood in front of his legs, not touching him. I was too embarrassed to even look at him. My eyes were now puffy, face and neck red as a beet, chest heaving, breath catching in my throat.

"Do you see this?" he inquired, pointing at his computer screen.

I looked at his face in disbelief. Was he really going to try to sell me on another couple right now? I gawked at his audacity.

Lucas looked at me expectantly. So, I turned my attention to the screen. On it was what appeared to be hotel room accommodations and maps. I looked back at him, not understanding what I was supposed to make of this.

"I have to go to Columbia, South Carolina for a diving certification. I was thinking that we could go together and while I was in class, you could go visit your family. I know you must miss them." My jaw hit the ground internally.

"I-I don't know what to say right now. I-you-us?" I stuttered.

A smile formed at the corner of his mouth and worked its way to the other side.

He nodded, "I-You-Us, together, in Columbia for a weekend. Is that a yes?" he urged.

I flung myself onto him, squeezing his neck tightly.

"Yes! Oh my god! Wait..." I pulled away from him.

"What?" Lucas looked at me intensely.

"You aren't fucking with me, are you?" I inquired, holding my breath, waiting for the letdown.

"I am not fucking with you," he laughed.

"This is real life? Yes?" I beamed.

He nodded.

I threw myself back onto him, covering him in kisses.

"Okay, okay, okay. I-I nee–"

I stuck my tongue in his mouth, interrupting his sentence, kissing him with all the passion I could muster in my body. He swatted my ass to get my attention. I pulled away and hopped up, holding my rear end.

"Focus, Amber. I need for you to be ready tomorrow morning. We will be leaving before sunrise," he instructed.

"I will! I will! Thank you, oh my god. I am so excited." I gushed.

"Good, I'm glad," Lucas replied. "Go get packed," he commanded.

Beaming at him, I gave him another kiss and a long squeeze before leaving.

***

I arrived at home on cloud nine. I reached out to my family to ensure a visit was okay and that it worked out with their schedule. I hung up the phone and squealed, spun around the room, and fell onto my bed laughing hysterically. As I flung myself onto my bed, the phone flew across the room, hit the wall, and crashed to the floor. I panicked for a moment, but decided *Fuck it, for now. I am enjoying this divine moment.*

I was going to see my relatives!

I was going to have an entire weekend away with my god!

Oh my god!

I calmed myself after a while and hopped up to check on my phone. The screen was cracked pretty severely. I turned on some music from my playlist to check the speakers. Sure enough, the speakers crackled and rattled.

"Fuck!" I said aloud.

I shot Lucas a text to see if anything else was impacted.

"Dropped my phone, cracked the screen and messed up the speakers. I'm going to have to get a new phone because I don't think I can hear anyone if they call."

My phone buzzed, "I have a spare you can use. I'll give it to you tomorrow morning. See you then. Are you packing?" he replied.

I smiled, "Thank you and YES!" I texted back.

Lucas sent back a wink face.

I gushed and put my phone down, so I could begin packing.

One hour later, I was packed and lying in bed wide awake, mind spinning with thoughts of seeing my family, their smiling faces, feeling their hugs, seeing their smiles... It melted my heart.

Thoughts then shifted to the possibilities of what it would be like to travel with Lucas, to spend the night in a bed by his side, to sleep–literally sleep–with him, to wake up to his face.

The notion of sleep was futile. So, I lay awake until my alarm went off. I dressed quickly and quietly, as the household was still asleep. I went with a natural beauty look, effortlessly beautiful. Spritzed on some perfume, shoved it into my bag, woke my mother to tell her I was heading out for the weekend, and disappeared out the door.

Lucas handed me a blue cell phone when I got into the truck.

"Take care of this, please. Do not answer any calls unless the calls are specifically for you. The passcode for voicemail is 2133, in case you miss a call," he instructed.

"Got it and I will take care of it, thank you."

* * *

We arrived at our hotel in the afternoon, checked in, got situated, and headed out for a bite to eat. I texted my family to let them know I was borrowing a cell phone until mine was replaced and that I had made it to Columbia. We set up a time for the following afternoon to spend time together. Plans were solidified over dinner between Lucas and me. He would drop me off at my cousin's house and go attend his scuba class. Later, he would pick me up and we would have dinner and quality time back at the hotel. Sunday, we would check out at 11 AM and head back to the beach.

32

Chapter 32

After we had our fill of food and a few drinks, Lucas and I headed back to our room. I flopped down on the bed, taking it all in. This was real life; I had traveled with this man, we were sharing a hotel room, he was doing all the things he does to prepare for a shower, and I got to witness it. Gratitude would not be adequate enough an adjective to describe how I was feeling; Awe and gratitude. I didn't truly understand how deeply I had been desiring to experience normalcy with Lucas until, here we were… occupying the same space, for two whole nights, sharing meals, a vehicle, a bathroom–

… A bed

The thought made me smile. Lucas kissed me on the forehead before disappearing into the bathroom for his shower. *This is amazing*, I squealed inside. I was giddy with excitement.

Twenty minutes later, the shower turned off. I listened to the silence. Some clicks, rustling around, then silence. The door opened, and there he stood; towel around his waist, steam clearing behind him. *Fuck me!* I screamed inside and bit the inside of my cheek.

"All yours, darlin," Lucas nodded his head back toward the bathroom.

"Is it now?" I replied cheekily, sauntering over and pressing my body into him.

We grinned at one another.

"Mmmm," he replied into my lips as I peeled my shirt off.

I lay a sexy, teasing kiss on his lips before patting his chest and brushing past him. He gave my ass a firm slap as I passed him, and I giggled. I decided to take a bath first and shave my legs and other parts. I wanted to be my absolute best for Lucas. I ran a heavenly bubble bath, sank down into it, and soaked for a few moments. I began shaving, and my thoughts flitted about, little fantasies about what awaited me when I got out of the tub, clean shaven, slick curvy body, standing before the gorgeous man that awaited me in the next room, completely nude.

I must've been so lost in thought that I failed to hear Lucas slip into the bathroom. I saw a shadow pass over the shower curtain, it began to rustle, and then it pulled back slightly. I was frightened at first, but quickly comprehended that is was my god. And he had a camera. I snatched the shower curtain back closed. My heart raced.

"Please don't film me," I asked, trying to use the calmest voice I could muster.

"Why? What's wrong with it?" he inquired.

I was feeling terribly upset and frightened by the prospect of my face and body being filmed.

"I-I'm sorry, you just surprised me. But I really don't want to be on camera," I explained.

"Please?" Lucas asked softly, still advancing and tugging at the shower curtain.

The camera appeared around the shower liner. I cringed down into the corner of the tub, as far away from it as I could. I made myself as covered and small as possible.

"Please don't do that, Lucas! I told you I don't want to!"

I felt myself coming unhinged and attempts to remain kind and to steady my voice and keep myself soft, were failing.

He snatched the curtain back, revealing me covering myself and cowering in the far corner of the tub.

"Why were you bathing with the shower curtain closed, anyway?"

I remained still, feeling uncomfortably vulnerable and exposed, embarrassed, and teetering between feeling ridiculous for how I was responding to this and feeling hurt that he had continued to try and film me even though he knew I didn't want it.

"Hey, it's okay. I won't show any pictures or videos that I take to anyone else. They are for our eyes only. Plenty of couples in the lifestyle do this. It's hot, and we can always go back through them together if we want. All of the X-Rated photos I take get locked in my safe, and only I have access to it," he carried on, trying to ease my aversion to being filmed.

"Please?" he pleaded softly.

I remained motionless, holding my breasts with one hand and covering my vagina with the other.

"Fine," I agreed, to appease him. "Just not in here, okay? I really would like to finish shaving and washing, you know? I'd like to be clean and looking beautiful."

I attempted to compose myself.

"That's my good girl."

Lucas grabbed my arm and pulled me to him, kissing me deeply. When he pulled away to look at me, I smiled the best I could to reassure him that we were fine, despite the fact that I felt like I was crumbling, fragile, slighted...

"Don't be long," he said as he left the bathroom.

Once the door had closed, I let out and audible exhale. I hadn't realized I had been holding my breath and didn't know for how long. I covered my mouth with one hand and clutched my throat with the other. I was in full-blown panic. I reminded myself to take some deep breaths, in through my nose and out through my mouth. It helped some, so I stepped out of the tub after finishing up and dried off.

I knew he was expecting me naked, so I opened the bathroom door and stepped out, presenting myself to him.

He lay on the bed on his back, his legs were spread shoulder width apart. I stood at the end of the bed, awaiting permission to climb aboard.

"Come here to me." Lucas gave the command.

I bit the inside of my bottom lip and pressed my knees and palms into the bed, crawling up to him. I arrived at his hips, straddling him. The room was dead silent and dark with the exception of the moonlight shining silver down my back, and creating silhouettes over his cheekbones, nose, and honey brown eyes. I tilted my head, to allow the light to illuminate his face, and admired how incredibly handsome he was below me. I loved the way it made me feel when he looked at me, like really looked at me… It didn't happen as often as it did when we had first met, but when it did, I wallowed in it like a dog in their favorite stench; with the utmost fervor and passion.

Using the back of his hand, Lucas lightly caressed my arm, my collar bone, my breasts, my stomach, and stopped at my hips, giving them an exquisite squeeze. I leaned over, giving him better access to my ass, and on cue, he took two handfuls of my rear end and squeezed, spreading me apart, my hips grinding into his, my pussy beginning to throb. Desiring his presence inside of me, I bit my bottom lip and smiled devilishly. Twisting my hips playfully and shaking my ass, I felt him becoming aroused.

"Mm," I moaned softly. "I want you," I stated softly.

Lucas bit his lip and smiled, "Do you?"

His voice was deep and calm. His hands roamed my body. I sat upright and took his hands, placing them on my breasts.

Sliding my pussy up and down the length of his hardening cock, I cooed seductively, "I want to please you."

I placed his left hand on my heart.

He allowed it, so I continued.

"May I… please you…Sir?"

It tumbled awkwardly from my mouth. I was determined to not allow myself to be self-conscious. I saw the question all the way through, and now, here we were, in this moment together, my request hanging in the air, in a very similar way to the moment I had admitted to being in love with him, my fragile, my vulnerable hanging out, wishing with all of its might to be said yes to, to be given permission to exist in a safe, judgement free space, to have a home to claim.

Let me in, let me in-

"Let me in," he spoke softly.

So, I placed him inside of me; we both gasped and our bodies tensed and shook.

"Fuck," I cried out, my voice hoarse from holding back the weeping that desired to purge itself from my lungs, the wailing that threatened to breech his boundaries.

I placed his left hand on my throat and squeezed it just hard enough that it was only slightly difficult to breath. And, my soul sighed, *Okay, I will abide.*

33

Chapter 33

Lucas raised up and we clung to one another, rocking back and forth. Our moans sounded incredible together, the most beautiful harmony. We were, we were... god; we were beautiful in those moments. He flipped me over onto my back, pulling my legs around him. Before he placed himself inside of me again, he hovered above me, looking into my eyes. A tender ferocity, I saw need, this was Lucas allowing some of his vulnerable to hang out. He caressed my cheek, my jaw, and then brushed the hair that was stuck to my face away gently. Lucas gazed into my eyes, stroking my face as though I were precious and beloved to him. I could feel his love, his tenderness, but more palpable than anything, was his need. Something had happened that I was unaware of. A shift...

Lucas pressed his forehead against mine and held me tightly to him as he pushed inside of me. He slid in slowly, his body doing that tremble thing that drove me fucking wild.

"Fuck," I whispered into his lips.

He moaned softly and held himself inside of me for a minute. He wrapped me up in what I considered to be 'a cocoon.' Arms around the top of my head, fingers clasped together, legs tangled in mine, and he began moving in and out of me slowly, slowly... He pulled almost all the way out and then slammed into me and held himself there, his body tensed. I could feel his muscles contracting. Something magical was happening here. I was pretty certain my god was indeed … making love to me.

Again and again, he pulled out slowly, and slammed into me. The orgasms I experienced from the suspense and impact were incredibly intense. His movements deliberate and calculated, he held my hands above my head and buried his face in the space between my shoulder and neck. I could smell his cologne, his body was slightly damp from sweat, and his breath on my neck paired with the slower tempo of this session had my mind in varied degrees of fucked up. *If he didn't want me to love him, why fuck me like this? This was only making me fall for him harder. I can't see this man's fragility and not rip my own heart out to give to him so that he hurts and hungers no more. Does he know this? He couldn't possibly.* The thoughts raced and bounced around in my brain.

I decided to ponder it all at a later time and tuned back in to what was happening. Lucas raised himself up and pulled my legs over his forearms; it was time to shift into high gear. He pushed into me forcefully; this was the beast that I recognized.

"Mm," I moaned. "Yes, yes," I whispered with every in-stroke.

He was quiet, focused, and I could tell he wanted to orgasm but was denying himself. Lucas fucked me properly for quite a while before settling back down, body to body atop me. He wrapped me up again in that heavenly cocoon. I nibbled at his jawline and neck.

His strokes became more intense and feverish. I could feel his cock hardening, preparing to orgasm. It was going to happen any second.

"I'm gonna… fuck-ugh! I'm gonna cum," Lucas spat out breathlessly.

"Yes, please cum, please-please," I responded, my pussy clamping down around him.

"Fuck!"

He gritted his teeth and slammed into me hard, his body spasming. His hips thrusting of their own accord until he lay still on top of me.

"Goddamn," he whispered, trying to catch his breath.

I lay there, my mind and skin buzzing with fuzzy warm feelings. My mind was still chewing on this new tender side of Lucas in the bedroom. I had to ask, or it would drive me entirely insane.

"C-can I ask you a question?" I began.

"Of course, what is it?" he replied.

"What just happened?" I blurted out.

He looked at me with a confused expression.

"Uh, what do you mean what just happened?" Lucas retorted.

I squeezed my eyes closed and held my temples to keep my brain from exploding.

"I mean, what was that... what you did, what we did? Lucas, it felt...," I paused to take a deep breath to steady myself. "It felt a lot like you just made love to me," I finished.

There, it was out and in the open. It didn't have to ping pong around inside of me anymore. I felt better.

He got quiet for a moment.

"Amber, don't," Lucas requested sternly.

I stared at him, fuming inside. *I know what the fuck I felt. You fucking made love to me, I know you did,* I argued in my head. He looked over at me, grabbed my arm and pulled me close. He patted his shoulder for me to place my head there. I snuggled in, lay my head on his shoulder, and allowed him to wrap my arm around his waist. I digressed and let the subject drop. He fell asleep pretty quickly; I, on the other hand, lay awake into the wee morning hours, replaying every minute detail to try and debunk the reality of the experience Lucas and I had shared.

At some point, I dropped off to sleep. We awoke to his alarm clock. I showered, dressed, and ate a meal on the way to my family's home to get dropped off. Lucas and I didn't speak much. He seemed to be a bit quiet first thing in the morning, perhaps not much of a morning person. Whatever the reason, I was determined to enjoy family time and reconvene with him later. I leaned in for a kiss before getting out of the truck at my cousin's house. Lucas kissed my cheek. I gawked at this sudden dynamic change in horror.

"I'll see you tonight," he said, staring straight ahead.

His voice was disinterested and slightly annoyed sounding.

"Are you okay?" I inquired.

"Yep," he replied curtly.

My eyebrows furrowed down in confusion.

"Are-um, we okay?" I pushed gently.

"I'm going to be late. I have to get going. We can discuss later, okay? Enjoy your family time."

Lucas shut down the question and answer session. I stared a moment longer and then vacated the truck, closing the door a little extra hard, instantly regretting my actions, and promptly apologizing for it as he pulled away.

Great, just fucking wonderful, I thought and waved a hand of dismissal to the bumper of Lucas'

Diesel. I did my best to move through the day with my family with a smile on my face. But I was deeply affected by the shift in our situation. By the time Lucas came to pick me up that evening, I was exhausted. Trying to pretend that I was 'fine,' putting on a show for my family, over-thinking what it was that he and I were going to discuss tonight, it killed me.

Lucas and I pulled into a restaurant.

"You hungry?" he inquired. "I know I am starving!" he added.

"I could eat," I replied quietly.

He hopped out of the truck and came around to my side, opened the door, helped me out, closed the door behind me, and placed his hand on the small of my back, leading me into the establishment.

My senses dulled due to a deep sadness that had curled itself around my heart, I couldn't really quite enjoy what typically was one of the million little things he did. Once seated, we scanned our menus, ordered, and sat in silence for what seemed like forever.

Lucas broke the silence, "I told you that we would talk today, before we went to sleep last night."

I nodded, pushing my food around my plate. He stared at me, and then to my plate, and then back to my face.

"Amber, look at me," he commanded gently.

I complied, looking up at him, unable to hide the sadness in my eyes; it had consumed me. I blinked to keep the tears at bay and tossed my hair away from my face.

We looked into one another's eyes for a moment before he spoke again.

"I want you to start seeing other people. You should find someone that is going to love you deeply and that you can give all of your love to."

My heart sank into my knee caps. I closed my eyes, holding my head back, hands hanging limply in my lap, and took in a deep breath. Lucas looked at me with concern.

"I know this is too much for you, what we are doing. I know you have feelings for me, despite the fact that I warned you against it. This is what needs to happen, Amber," he explained.

Bringing my head back to face forward, I looked at him, eyes misted over, bottom lip quivering.

"Are-are you saying this because…" The lump in my throat was making it impossible to speak, so I swallowed and took in a breath through my nose. "Are you saying this because I am never going to see you again, after we get home?"

I held my breath, awaiting his response.

"No," he replied softly. "I am saying this because I truly feel it is best that you find someone to love you, and someone in whom you can invest your love. You have so much to offer the right person, Amber."

"I don't need you to lecture me on what you think is best for me, Lucas," I spat out, feeling resentful.

I pushed my plate away from me and sat back, crossing my arms. He shook his head disapprovingly.

"Amber, don't do this," he urged, looking annoyed.

"Don't do what, Lucas?" I hissed, leaning forward. "Embarrass you with my feelings?"

I stared him down before sitting back in my seat.

"Fine…" I continued.

He looked at me, confused.

"You want me to see other people? I will," I threatened, scanning his face for any reaction; he gave none.

"You need to eat." Lucas nodded toward my food, pushing it back toward me.

If looks could have killed, he would've been 100 feet under the ground in that moment. I sat there in defiance for a couple of minutes. He proceeded to eat his meal. I unwrapped my silverware from the napkin, placed the napkin in my lap, served him the most annoyed face I could muster, picked up my fork, and began eating my meal.

34

Chapter 34

The ride home was a silent one. I don't think either of us really knew what to say to the other. I was flip flopping back and forth between internal dialogues and evil plans. One side of me screamed and cried about my broken heart, the other side of me tossed her hair and flipped Lucas the middle finger; my truth lay somewhere in the midst of all of this chaos. The roaring of my head and heart at war was too loud to discern anything at the moment, so I allowed them to fight and rage on. We pulled into my neighborhood. I pulled my bag into my lap, clutching it tightly, secretly wishing I could just open the door and fling myself out that very second; anything had to feel better than this bullshit.

Lucas parked in front of the curb just outside my house. As quickly as he had put the truck in park, I opened the door to exit. He pulled at the back of my shirt to get my attention. I turned to face him, our eyes locked, and I noticed a slight sadness. We sat in silence for several minutes, once again, neither of us knowing what to say.

"Here is your phone, thank you for letting me use it."

I pulled his phone from my pocket.

Lucas pushed my hand back, "No, keep it until you get a new phone. We will need a way to stay in touch."

I gawked at him, confused.

"Darlin', I didn't say we couldn't see each other anymore. I said you need to see other people, find someone that loves you and that you can love in return. I can't be that person for you," he explained.

I slid the phone into the side pocket of my bag.

What he failed to realize is that I didn't want to fall in love with anyone else. He was my person, my heart chose him out of all the others that might be better suited, for rather dull reasons. Something inside of me just fucking decided it didn't matter what struggles may come, no matter what people thought or said... no matter what he thought or said, my heart had decided that I was to love him with every fiber of my being, no negotiating, no second guessing, it was not an option. What he failed to realize was that if I were to, by very slim chances, fall madly and deeply for another, I didn't possess the capacity to hold space in my heart for both; that if I fell in love with another, he/we would be no more. I didn't want that. I chose him. I just wished more than anything that he would choose me back. And it hurt like hell every time he didn't; every single fucking time... The sacrifices I was making and would make just to hear him say he loved me and mean it were great. I would do things for this man that I would do for no other.

I looked at the floorboard, fidgeting with my fingers.

"How does this work? Am I supposed to like, just go on dates and stuff? Do I tell you if I am going to go out with someone? Do I not tell you? I don't know what I am supposed to do anymore, Lucas. And, all of this... things that used to make sense just don't make sense to me. I'm..." I threw my hands in the air and let them fall limply onto my bag.

Lucas stared straight ahead, his jaw tensed.

"Never mind. I'm sorry. I'm unloading on you and you probably don't want to deal with it. I'm just gonna go. Sorry to bother you with my shit," I said, feeling completely and utterly defeated and lost.

"It's not like that, Amber. We are friends and you can talk to me about things; I just can't allow you to fall in love with me. Do you understand that?" he inquired.

I laughed a sarcastic laugh, "You're a little late to the party, Lucas. I fell in love with you the moment I laid eyes on you. But that's not your issue to contend with. This is something that, obviously, I have to deal with by myself. I'll do my best, from here on out, to not make my feelings for you continue to be a problem, and I will do my best to keep them contained so that you aren't made to feel uncomfortable. As fucking pathetic as it is, I would rather have you in my life as something, than for us to be nothing at all. I will take you as you will allow me to have you."

I mentally punched myself in the face for saying that out loud. But I stood by it, I meant it, it was the ugly truth.

"What would make you feel more comfortable? Do you want to tell me if you are going to go on a date or are seeing someone? Either way is fine." Lucas spoke softly, redirecting the conversation.

I pondered his questions carefully.

Shrugging, I responded, "I don't know. I guess I'd feel better if I let you know what was going on so that, maybe, everyone was on the same page?"

Lucas nodded, "If that would make you feel more comfortable then that is fine with me."

I mulled this over, and shook my head, agreeing. "I think I should do that. I'll tell you."

"You can send me a picture so that I can make sure you don't fuck some ugly loser; your first line of defense," he quipped.

My eyes bugged out of my head. I wasn't sure if I was more offended that he thought my standards were that low or that he was so comfortable making such an incredulously horrendous joke in a moment of fragility. I blinked furiously in an attempt to wrap my mind around the fact that this had just happened. In an effort to deliver the moment from impending explosion, I smiled—to protect him from my breaking heart. I even managed a quiet laugh. One day, I would be good at this faking it stuff, I hoped.

"Okay, um—I am going to get going. When will I hear from you again?" I inquired.

"I will be pretty busy for the next while, but we will be in touch. Send me a text and check in every now and again, darlin," he replied casually.

I nodded, tucking my hair behind my ear. "Right... will do." Attempting to be super casual in my exchange with him.

I was going to need a fuck ton of practice in order to ever be even remotely comfortable with the process of stuffing my feelings down around him. Lucas pulled me to him and kissed me. Welcome to my own personal level of hell, the 7th gate, the torturous place of crumbling, numbing, far awayness. We hope you enjoy your stay in Disassociationland, population 1.

The emotional labor of love and trauma are both one in the same. The same amount of effort and self-loathing are required to sustain them.

35

Chapter 35

Over a two-month span, my and Lucas' communication was limited. I reached out a handful of times to check in. I had made some major changes in my life. I had moved out of my mom's house and was living on my own, had a car of my own, was working at a resort on the ocean-front as a receptionist. In essence, a complete life overhaul. I had made friends with my coworkers and we would all hang out after our shift until the wee morning hours. I still thought of him constantly. He consumed most of my thoughts, in all reality. I functioned because I had to. Going out dancing helped, the occasional stranger that would scoop me up or press his body tight to mine while on the dance floor. It broke my heart, but I closed my eyes and imagined it was Lucas. And it never felt quite right, so I drank myself into a stupor every night.

I lived for the times he responded to my texts, which the chances of that happening had become more and more unlikely. I listened to a voicemail from a number that had called while I was holding the phone one day, praying he would just call… It was a woman named Laura, and she was sobbing and begging him to just call her back. She swore she'd do anything he wanted if he would just talk to her. My heart broke for her; I knew all too well that she was one of his many. I knew how she felt, because, so would I. I'd do anything too. *Laura, it will never be enough. Get some sleep.*

Some alarming things had begun happening to my body. I thought that, perhaps, I was just stressed and exhausted from the life I had been living for months now that made my period late. My breasts were also tender in a very different way than was typical before my period started. I was at work one evening and had to catch myself on the counter so that I didn't fall into the floor. I grew dizzy and my vision went black. I felt like I was going to throw up. So, my boss sent me home. On my way home, I decided to stop at the store for some cold and flu medicine. As I browsed the aisles, I passed condoms, lube, and pregnancy tests.

My stomach lurched as it dawned on me that I may be pregnant. I passed by them and moved on to choose my medicine, adamantly denying that this could be possible. Unable to now get this notion out of my head, I went back to the pregnancy tests. I stared at them for a good twenty minutes, debating. The only option was to buy three tests. Because sometimes these things can be wrong. I checked out and went into the bathroom. Ripping into the box, I unwrapped everything and sat on the toilet, holding my pee, staring at this thing in my hand.

"I can't be pregnant. Can I?"

I felt the panic rising. Taking in a deep breath, I placed the stick between my legs and released my urine.

I watched the pee soak into the test strip. A line appeared, I reread the instructions, one line not pregnant, two lines pregnant.

"Okay, so far only one line. So, I'm not pregnant. Okay..."

I breathed a sigh of relief. I tossed the test into the metal trash container in the stall. I was just about to toss the box when I read the instructions also stated that I must wait for 3-5 minutes for accurate results.

I squeezed my eyes closed and mumbled, "Fuck."

Pulling the test back out of the trash can, I begrudgingly looked down at it. Two lines. My heart stopped. *No... Nope. Nope... No. Mm mm. The test is wrong. I can't be pregnant. Lucas said he had the surgery and after my son from my previous marriage was born, the doctors had said that it wouldn't be likely that I would ever be able to conceive again! I screamed inside. These things can be faulty. Yes, it is a fluke. A bad test. That's why I bought more. I'll take another one, and it'll show that I am most definitely not pregnant.*

I strained out the little urine I had left onto the second test stick. I waited for five minutes and looked at the result. It was positive.

"Oh Jesus… Oh shit… Oh god… Oh no. Okay…" I breathed.

I was officially freaking the fuck out. I called my best friend in Columbia, South Carolina. She picked up on the third ring.

"Hola Chica. What's up?"

I was silent. I couldn't begin to fathom what I was supposed to say in this moment. I think more than anything I just needed to have someone sit in silence with me in that bathroom stall.

"Amber? You there? Hello?" Tabitha pressed.

"I-yeah. Um…" I stuttered.

"Amber, what's going on? You okay?"

I sat in silence for another thirty seconds.

"No. I'm not okay," I said in a grave tone.

"Are you in danger? Where are you? What's going on, honey?"

I began to tear up.

"I'm pregnant." I whispered, my voice quivering.

"WHAT?" Tabitha yelled into the phone. "Is-" she began.

I cut her off because I knew what she was going to ask. "Yes, Lucas is the father."

Tabitha gasped. "Honey, do you know for sure?" she inquired.

I nodded as if she could see me nodding through the phone. "Yes, I took two tests." I replied.

"Fuck meeee!" she exclaimed. "I thought that-" Tabitha began.

I cut her off again, "Me too. He told me he had the surgery and that he couldn't get anyone pregnant. And then there is me; like, I don't get it. The doctors said I'd never have another child. What the fuck am I going to do, Tabby? Oh my god…"

I shoved my forehead in my free hand.

"No, no, no… Don't do that, Amber. Don't cry, honey. We will get through this together, okay? Where are you right now?" she attempted to calm me down.

"I'm sitting on the toilet at Wal-Mart."

My pants were still around my ankles, knees pressed together, holding my forearm and head.

"Okay, straighten yourself out. Go get another test. I am on my way to you. Go home, and don't do anything or make any decisions until I get there. I will see you in three hours," Tabitha instructed.

I nodded my head. "Okay. I already have a test for the house," I replied.

"Perfect, okay, so, don't take it until I get there. I'll be there as soon as I can get there. I love you. Go home, okay?" she urged.

"I will. I love you too. Thank you," I said weakly.

36

Chapter 36

The time in between me making it home and Tabitha arriving was a blur. I lost hours of time. One moment, I was sitting on the edge of my bed, hands palm down on my knees, staring blankly at the walls of my bedroom; the next moment, Tabby was rushing in the door.

"Amber?"

I snapped out of the trance I was in. She appeared in the doorway. We stared at each other, my bottom lip began to quiver.

"Oh honey… Come here!"

I sprang from the bed and we clung to one another, swaying side to side.

"I love you, I'm here okay?" Tabitha pulled away from me and brushed the hair out of my face. "You hear me? We will get through this together, okay?"

I nodded, tears streaming down my face.

"Let's get this other pregnancy test done. You know, sometimes, they can be wrong."

She ushered me into the bathroom. I pulled my pants down, Tabby clutched my free hand while I peed on the third and final pregnancy test.

"Don't look at it yet. Let's wait like the instructions say, okay? Wash up, put some cold water on your face. We got this. No matter what, you will be just fine. Do you know that?"

I didn't answer. I pulled my pants up, washed up, dried my face with the hand towel, and carried the test out into my room.

Sitting on the edge of the bed, the two of us looked at everything except for the pregnancy test for five minutes. The timer that Tabby had set went off. We looked at one another and then turned our attention to the test I clutched in my hands. She nodded at me to uncover it. I opened my hands; the test was positive. There was no way around it, no denying it, I was pregnant. Tabitha grabbed me, wrapped her arms around me and I fell over, falling apart; weeping and sobbing, hyperventilating.

"Oh my god, Tabby," I wailed.

"Oh, honey. Shh, sh… I'm here. I'm here with for, for you. You won't do this alone. And no matter what you decide, I will support you." She encouraged me and stroked my hair.

The sobs turned to sniffling and body jerks. The tears were still streaming but I was calming down. I took in a deep shuddering breath. Tabitha rubbed my back and then squeezed me tightly. I was coming around to understanding that this was indeed happening. This was my reality, and I needed to figure out how I was going to make this work. Tabitha snuggled into the curve between where my shoulder meets my neck, moved my hair out of the way and spoke softly into my ear, "You are going to be a mommy."

I couldn't quite understand, nor did I really want to try to break down the spectacular shift that happened in this moment. I began beaming and sobbing all at the same time. A voice in my spirit said, *You will not be alone in this, because I am with you. You are more capable and braver than you know; what may come, we will face with strength and dignity.* I rolled over and squeezed Tabitha back. I started laughing hysterically and crying all at the same time.

We sat up and I said, "I'm going to be a mommy."

We beamed at each other and I touched my stomach and then so did she.

"Yes, you are. And a damn fine one," she replied.

I nodded, agreeing.

"Not to be the bearer of actual bad news, but… have you told Lucas?" Tabby inquired, eyebrows raised with worry.

I shook my head no. She took in a deep breath.

"Okay… Okay! So, let's make sure we get that out of the way. Call him now? Ask him to talk?" she suggested gently.

"Yes," I replied and pulled his contact information up.

The phone rang twice, and Lucas picked up, "Sure-Clean, this is Lucas,"

I froze. I searched Tabitha's face for the words.

She nodded, "You've got this… Tell him you need to talk," she urged quietly.

"I-I need to talk to you, Lucas. It's very important. It's an emergency, in fact," I replied.

There was silence on Lucas' end. I could tell he was trying to decipher the nature of 'said emergency,' he was waiting for me to explain myself. But I didn't.

"Sure, what's up?" he finally spoke.

"No, this isn't something that we need to discuss on the phone. I need you to meet with me; preferably sooner than later."

I looked to Tabitha for support. She smiled and nodded her approval.

"Um, okay," Lucas replied hesitantly. "I am nearby, I can meet you in ten minutes in the parking lot of that little pancake place by your house?" he continued.

"That's fine. I'll be there. See you then."

And, I hung up.

"Good job, honey. You did so good. You stay strong, do you hear me? Do you need for me to go with you? Do you think he would do anything to hurt you or the baby?" Tabitha questioned.

I shook my head, "I don't think he would physically harm me. As far as how breaking the news to him is going to go," I shrugged my shoulders. "As far as how he is going to respond, that is up for debate as well. It is anyone's guess. I can just hope for the best, you know?" I replied.

"Yeah, that's kinda all you can do right now. Make sure you call me if you need me. And I'll come kick his ass."

Tabby made a fist and shook it at me.

I laughed, "I will."

She nodded, and I hugged her goodbye. My mind was strangely quiet the short trip to meet with Lucas. I got out of my car and into his truck. I sat there, my hands glued to the leather seat. He stared at me expectantly.

"What's going on?"

I looked down at the floorboard, "I'm pregnant."

I pressed my lips together and waited for his reaction. As per usual, he stared straight ahead, jaw tensed, and a vein popped out at his temple. We sat in silence for several minutes.

"It's not mine," he replied, his voice deep and stern.

My jaw hit the ground, my eyes widened. I was so blown away that I couldn't speak.

"Uh, yes, this baby is yours!" I screeched at him.

His jaw tightened even more, "Not possible. I had the surgery. I've been fixed."

I narrowed my eyes at him, feeling enraged.

"Well, might I suggest a new doctor and that you go back, and have it redone because it didn't fucking work."

Lucas swung his head my way. "It's not mine."

I began laughing, I wanted to punch him right in his mouth.

"Why do you keep calling the baby IT? This child is yours."

He went back to staring straight ahead, "How do I know that?"

My jaw hit the ground again.

"Are you fucking kidding me right now? I've only been sleeping with you!"

I was losing my cool.

"Again, how do I know that?" he retorted smugly.

I took in a deep breath and licked my lips. It was taking every bit of restraint that I had to not go ape shit on him. I sat there, staring at him, envisioning how good it would feel to beat the shit out of him, and then decided that it would be counter-productive to the goal here, which was to tell him we were going to have a child and see what he was going to do. *Focus, keep it together, Amber*, I coached myself.

"Are you going to keep it?" Lucas inquired.

I leaned toward the window on my side, unable to fathom that what I was hearing and seeing was real life.

"Of course, I am going to keep, THE BABY," I raised my voice.

"Keep in mind that I offered an option and you refused then."

My eyes bugged out of my head.

"Abortion? That's your 'offering,' your solution? To murder our child? Abortion isn't a fucking option," I snapped.

He said nothing, wouldn't look at me, no reaction, just stone faced.

"So that's it? This is what it's going to be? I'm doing this alone?" I flung question after question at him.

He sighed, "I'm too old to be a fuckin' father, Amber!" He raised his voice to me.

My eyebrows shot up.

He looked at me, "I can't be a father. My wife, my kids, everything… ruined, gone, done. This would end me; don't you get that? My children—it would destroy them. I can't do it, Amber. Fuck!"

He slammed his fist on the steering wheel. I jumped, squeezing my eyes shut.

"Please don't do that," I requested quietly.

We sat in silence.

"Look, I won't say anything to your family. I didn't come here to tell you about this because I wanted to cause a problem. I was hoping that…"

I got quiet, feeling bad, guilty; it shook me and broke my resolve. What I was so steadfast in upon getting into Lucas' truck was unstable and crumbling.

His face fell, "I can't do this… I can't." His voice was weak. He shook his head. I looked down at the floorboard, fidgeting with my fingers.

"Okay..." I said.

Lucas looked at me. I looked back at him.

"Okay, I promise I won't tell anyone. I'm sorry. I'm sorry. I'll do this by myself. I won't bother you."

I handed him his phone back.

"Laura called, by the way," I added.

He looked at me, surprised.

"Laura?" he repeated.

I nodded, "Yes, she seemed pretty upset that you weren't calling her back. She said she would do anything just to have you call her back," I said in a flat tone.

Lucas laughed and shook his head, "She is a submissive I went out with a few times, she's desperate."

My heart broke again for her. I was beginning to grasp a clearer understanding of this enigma of a man.

"She sounded pretty sad to me, maybe you should call her," I defended her.

"Phhhfftt," Lucas huffed, waving a dismissive hand. "She's pathetic. Fucked her good a few times and now I can't get rid of her."

I nodded my head, "Well, that's all that I needed to tell you. I'll figure it out on my own. I just thought you should know," I said, heartbroken and nauseated.

I exited the truck and drove home on autopilot. Tabitha was waiting for me, biting her nails when I walked in.

"You okay? How'd it go?" she fired questions.

"I think I'm okay, I mean—as okay as I can be given the circumstances, you know?" I shrugged.

"Well, yeah... But what happened? Is he going to help you take care of the baby?"

I looked at the floor.

"That mother fucker..."

Tabitha knew from the look on my face.

I shrugged again, "I told him I would figure it out by myself," I replied glumly.

Tabitha shook her head in disbelief, "You did what?"

"He kept calling the baby an IT, Tabby. He tried to get me to have an abortion. Apparently, he claims that he is, and I quote, 'too fucking old to be a father'. So, yeah… I'll be doing it on my own," I responded.

Tabitha was now holding her heart, her eyes bugged out of her head, "Take me to this mother fucker's office, Amber. Too fucking old to be a father, my ass. Tell me you are not going to allow him to do this to you?"

She narrowed her eyes at me and put her hands defiantly on her hips.

"Tabby, he is married, he has children, a little girl that thinks he hung the moon and stars! A wife, Tabby… I was helping him to cheat and now, I am pregnant. Do you know what would happen to him if anyone found out?" I explained.

I waited for her answer. She stared at me, wide-eyed, mouth open, her face and chest turning blood red.

"Ummm, what in the actual fuck? What has this guy done to your fucking head, Amber? Hello, is anyone in there?"

She made a knocking motion in the air. I rolled my eyes.

"You don't understand," I retorted, walking to the fridge for a bottled water.

Tabby just stood still, "Apparently, I don't…" she replied sarcastically. "Apparently, I am failing to understand how it is that you are defending this man, apologizing for being pregnant with his child, letting him off the hook, essentially. So, he has some kids, he also now has a child with you, and he should be responsible for this child, no?" she fumed.

"Tabby, please…," I spoke softly, urging her to drop it.

She shook her head disapprovingly, "This guy has your head all sorts of fucked up. I can only pray that, one day, you come to your senses and you realize both your and this baby's worth. Because, right now, you're allowing that mouth breathing piece of shit to walk all over you. I can't fucking believe you are defending him. Amber, you are a stronger woman than this, and I have to say, I am surprised. If you won't be upset and mad as hell for yourself, then I will be pissed the fuck off for you. I say this with love, honey. I love you, I do, but you're being a weak ass bitch, right now. A stupid ass bitch too, and you're one of the most intelligent, fiercest, most independent women I know, so that's fucking saying something," Tabitha ranted.

Tears started flowing again. I dropped my water bottle and covered my face.

"Shit... I'm sorry, Am..."

Tabitha rushed to me and wrapped me up, holding me.

"No, don't apologize," I began, between sobs. "You're right. I'm just really fucking confused, and scared, I jus—I..."

I couldn't finish my sentence.

"No, shh, shh, shh, honey. I can only imagine how terrified and confused you are right now. I just wanted to talk some sense into you. You aren't being yourself, you aren't thinking clearly. I know you just found out you're pregnant, and you're trying to sort out all of the shit, but you don't have to do it alone. And you shouldn't do it alone. Do you know that?" She rubbed my back.

I nodded, "I know. I'll figure it out. I'll fix it. I'm sorry," I replied.

Tabby grabbed my chin, "Why are you apologizing to me? You see, Am? This is the shit I am talking about... You, apologizing for being human, having feelings, apologizing for existing. That shit hurts my heart so badly for you, mama. This isn't the Amber that I know. It might take some time, but please, find you again because-" She stopped abruptly to take a deep breath and look deeply into my eyes. "Goddamn him," she seethed through gritted teeth and then grabbed my head and held me tightly to her chest. "I'll help you raise this baby," Tabitha promised.

37

Chapter 37

I was thirty-eight weeks along when I admitted myself into the hospital for a scheduled cesarean. 8AM on a chilly November morning, I lay on the table, guts splayed, doctors digging through muscle and tissue, pushing and pulling until 8:45 AM, when that magical moment that can never really fully be described happened; my baby's cry filled the hospital room. It was strong, healthy, and I cried right along with him. (I was sobbing) The nurses laid a perfect 6 pound 7 ounce baby boy on my chest. They beamed and told me he was beautiful.

"He is, isn't he?" I replied through the fog of drugs coursing through my system.

"I love you, thank you for choosing me, I am so happy you are here," I smiled and whispered to him, kissing his forehead, noses, and fingers.

I wasn't off the table yet, (out of the woods). Doctors were working hard to stitch and staple me back up. I wanted to make sure my son knew I loved him first and foremost, should the unthinkable happen. They took him from me, so they could run tests, and also so the doctors could get me on my way to recovery, with no distractions. I was calm, and as Tabby had so wonderfully and eloquently reminded me all those months ago, I remembered to not be a weak ass bitch. I had been quite strong, and I had been quite brave.

Close friends and family drove in from out of town to see us once I was stable enough to be moved into recovery. I was lucky enough to have a room to myself, and all of the quiet I needed to wrap my head around the fact that he was here, my beautiful, beautiful, perfect baby boy, whom also, by the way, had a marvelous set of lungs on him. The nurses gushed over him adoringly. My son was the only boy born on that day in the hospital, so they dubbed him, "The prince of the nursery." Tabitha arrived, balloons and gifts in hand. She peeked around the corner and beamed at me.

I smiled back, "Hey you."

She came in tip toeing, "Where is my Godson?"

I laughed and grabbed my incision. "Ow," I winced.

"Shit! I'm sorry. No laughing. Forbidden," she quipped, touching my hand gently.

I snickered again, this time, carefully.

"Seriously, though, where is the little guy? I demand to get my kisses in!" Tabitha pressed. "Nurses have him, running tests and doing their normally hospital stuff. He is wonderful, and so handsome," I gushed.

"Well, of course he is honey, look at how gorgeous his mother is," she replied.

I patted her hand, "Thank you… for being here, for being there all of those times."

I teared up.

"Do not cry, bitch, because I sure as hell will ruin this makeup job I did on myself, so that I don't scare my Godson the first time he sees me."

Tears formed in her eyes. We shared a careful laugh. Moments later, they brought him in. "There's my boy!" I reached my arms out and gave them the 'gimme' fingers.

"He is an absolute delight," the nurse said as she passed him to me.

"Yes, he is," I said, touching his tiny lip.

She gave an adoring look and left the room.

"My sweet boy meet your God mama, Tabby. Tabby, here is your Godson."

I passed him to Tabitha, who scooped him up from my arms as

carefully as I had ever seen anyone pick up a baby. Her face melted into a cross between serenity and absolute bliss. My heart melted too.

"You are so beautiful with him in your arms. You look so happy," I whispered.

She looked up from him and beamed at me, hugging him to her tightly.

"I am so happy for you, I am so in love with him, and I am so proud of you. Look what you did?" She smiled as a tear rolled down her cheek. "Fuck, I'm crying." Tabitha clasped her hand over her mouth. "Shit! I didn't mean to curse. I mean shoot. Don't repeat that. Don't do as Tabby does, peanut. I'm going to be a terrible Godmother."

She shook her head laughing.

I giggled, "We will be just fine, remember?"

Tabitha smiled endearingly at me, "Yes, we will. I love you."

"I love you too," I replied.

She handed him to me and kissed my forehead.

"Get some rest, you two. I'll try to stop back by before you get out, but if I can't, then please let me know when you are home and settled in. I'll see about coming for an extended visit to help you get adjusted, okay?" Tabitha reassured me.

"I will, and I'd like that a lot," I replied.

We said our goodbyes and she disappeared, leaving my son and me alone. I lay there, cuddling this human being that was now on the outside of my stomach, marveling at how magnificent he was. I realized I hadn't contacted Lucas to let him know he had arrived.

A few more friends and family arrived, they paid their respects, gifts, balloons, lots of diapers and the cutest onesies ever. The love was so beautiful and abundant from this small group of people, it made my heart feel so full. In this moment, I was fully happy, fully brave, and even though I was lying on a hospital bed, even though I had just had a human being literally pulled out of my body, even though I was cut open from hip bone to hip bone, I was strong. I picked up the hospital phone and dialed Lucas' number.

He picked up on the second ring, "Sure-Clean, this is Lucas."

"Hi," I said.

There was a brief pause.

"What number are you calling from?" he inquired.

"I am calling you from the hospital," I stated softly.

Another brief pause, "Well, what are ya doin' in the hospital?"

This time, the pause was mine.

"I just wanted to call you to let you know that our son was born today. We are here at Briarcliff Hospital, if you'd like to see him."

I hung up the phone and looked into my son's eyes, my heart breaking for him, knowing that his life was so complicated already.

"You will always have me, my sweet, sweet boy; no matter what, I will choose you every day, *every day*."

I kissed his forehead and snuggled him to my chest.

"It's you and me, kiddo. We got this."

To my knowledge, Lucas never visited our son at the hospital.

www.ingramcontent.com/pod-product-compliance
Lightning Source LLC
Chambersburg PA
CBHW021427110726
47901CB00008B/2335